Joseph Sheridan Le Fanu

The Rose and the Key

Vol. I

Joseph Sheridan Le Fanu

The Rose and the Key
Vol. I

ISBN/EAN: 9783337078850

Printed in Europe, USA, Canada, Australia, Japan

Cover: Foto ©Andreas Hilbeck / pixelio.de

More available books at **www.hansebooks.com**

ROSE AND THE KEY.

BY

J. SHERIDAN LE FANU,

AUTHOR OF "CHECKMATE," "UNCLE SILAS," "GUY DEVERELL," &c.

IN THREE VOLUMES.

VOL. I.

LONDON:

CHAPMAN AND HALL, 193, PICCADILLY.

1871.

LONDON:
PRINTED BY C. WHITING, BEAUFORT HOUSE, DUKE STREET,
LINCOLN'S-INN-FIELDS.

TO

THOMAS E. BEATTY, ESQ., M.D..
F.R.C.S.I.,

A NAME CELEBRATED IN HIS LEARNED AND BRILLIANT

PROFESSION ;

A GUILELESS AND GENIAL NATURE,

AND A

DELIGHTFUL COMPANION,

BELOVED, ADMIRED, AND HONOURED BY MANY FRIENDS,

AND

BY NONE MORE THAN BY THE AUTHOR,

THESE PAGES ARE

INSCRIBED WITH MUCH AFFECTION.

CONTENTS OF VOL. I.

THE ROSE AND THE KEY.

CHAPTER I.

UNOCULUS.

THE level light of a summer sunset, over a broad heath, is brightening its brown undulations with a melancholy flush, and turning all the stalks of heather in the foreground into twisted sticks of gold. Insect wings sparkle dimly in the air; the lagging bee drones homeward, and a wide drift of crows, cawing high and faint, show like shadows against the sea-green sky, flecked with faint crimson, as they sail away to the distant dormitories of Westwold Forest.

Toward the sunset end of this savage heath stand four gigantic fir-trees, casting long shadows.

One, indeed, is little more than a rotten stump, some twelve feet high; all bend eastwards, shorn of their boughs nearly to the top, and stretching the arms that remain, some yellow and stripped of their bark, in the same direction, as if signalling together to the same distant point. These slanting fir-trees look like the masts of a mighty wreck submerged; and antiquaries say that they are the monumental relics of a forest that lies buried under the peat.

A young lady, her dress of dark serge, with a small black straw-hat, a little scarlet feather in it, and wearing a pair of boots, such as a country artist might produce, made of good strong leather, with thick soles, but, in spite of coarse work and clumsy material, showing a wonderfully pretty little foot, is leaning lightly against one of these great firs. Her companion, an elderly lady, slight and merry, sits on a hillock of turf at her feet.

The dress of the elder lady corresponds with that of the younger. It is that of a person inured to the practice of a strict but not uncomfortable economy.

The young lady has dropped a japanned colour-box and a block-book at her feet. Is she an artist? Possibly a governess? At all events, she is one of the loveliest creatures eyes ever lighted on. Is there any light more becoming than that low and richly tinted, that comes subdued through the mists of sunset?

With a pleased look—the listening look which such spiritual delight assumes—with parted lips, the light touching the edge of her little teeth, with eyes a-glow with rapture, drinking in the splendour and beauty of the transitory hour and scene, as if she could look on in silence and beatitude for ever, the girl leans her little shoulder to the ancient tree.

With a long sigh, she says at last:

"I was going to ask your forgiveness, dear old cousin Max."

"For what?" asked the old lady, turning up a face pleasantly illuminated with the golden light which catches the tip of her nose and chin, and the edge of her good-natured old cheek.

"For making you take so long a walk. I'm a little tired myself. But I don't beg your pardon, because I think this more than makes amends. Let us look for a minute more, before all fades."

The old lady stood up, with a little shrug and screw of her shoulders.

"So I am—quite stiff—my old bones do complain; but oh, really, it is quite beautiful! I see it so much better standing here; that bank was in my way. How splendid—gorgeous!"

The scene was indeed worth a detour in their

homeward route. Two grand and distant ranges of mountain, approaching from right and left, stop short in precipitous terminations that resemble the confronting castles of two gigantic lines of fortification, leaving an undulating plane between, with the sunset sky, and piles of flaming cloud, for a horizon; and, in the comparatively near foreground, rises between these points an abrupt knoll crowned by the ruined castle of Cardyllion, and, with the village studded with grand old trees, looking like a town on fire.

In nearer foreground, in the hollow, in solemn purple shadow, are masses of forest; and against the faint green and yellow sky are spread streaks of purple vapour, and the fading crimson and scarlet fires of sunset.

"This should reconcile us to very humble ways; and more, I feel that through marble pillars, through great silk curtains, among mirrors, bronzes, china, and all the rest, looking out from a velvet sofa, I could not see, much less enjoy all this, as I do."

Cousin Max laughed.

"Very wise! very philosophical! very romantic!" exclaimed she. "But it is enough to be content with one's station in life, and not to grow too fond of any. To be content is, simply, not to wish for change. My poor father used to say that those, who wished for change were like those who wished for death. They longed for a state of which they had no experience, and for which they might not be so fit as they fancied, for every situation has its liabilities as well as its privileges. That is what he used to say."

"Dear Max, I withdraw it, if I said anything sensible, for whenever I do you grow so wise that you bore me to death." She kissed her. "Do let us be foolish, darling, while we are together, and we shall understand one another perfectly. See how quickly the scene changes. It is very beautiful, but not quite so glorious now."

At this moment the sound of steps, close behind them upon the soft peat, made them both turn their heads.

A sleek, lean man, lantern-jawed, in a shabby, semi-clerical costume, passed them by in front, from right to left, in an oblique line. He was following a path, and was twirling a stick slowly in his hand by its crooked handle, and gazing up at the sky with one eye—the other was blind—with a smile that was meant to be saintly. In spite of his meek smile, and his seedy and mean exterior, the two ladies had come to connect ideas of the sinister and the dangerous with this man.

"Gracious me!" said the elder lady, after a pause, "I do believe—I'm almost sure—that is the very man."

"I am perfectly certain," said the young lady, who had followed him with her eyes until he was hidden from view by a screen of furze and hawthorns, a little way to the left. "I can't imagine what that odious, ill-looking man can possibly mean by following us about as he does."

"Perhaps, after all, he is asking himself a question very like that about us?" said the old lady, with a laugh.

"Not he. He *is* following us."

"I saw him at Penmaen Mawr, but nowhere else," said Miss Max.

"But I saw him at Chester, and there could be no mistake about his watching us there. I saw him look at our luggage, and look for our names there, and I saw him stand on the step of his carriage at Conway, until he saw us get out with the evident intention of staying there; and then he got down with that little leather bag, that seems to be all that he possesses, and he came to our hotel, simply, I am certain, to watch us. You must recollect, when we returned from our walk, that I told you I saw him sitting in the room near the stairs, don't you recollect, writing—don't you remember?"

"Yes, I remember your saying there was a man

blind of an eye, the same we had observed at Penmaen Mawr, who had followed us, and was in the
same place. But the people at the inn said he was
a travelling secretary to some religious society,
collecting money."

"Did not you say," persisted the young lady,
"when you first saw him, that he was a very ill-
looking man?"

"Yes; so I did. So he is. He looks sancti-
monious and roguish, and that white eye makes his
face—I hope it is not very uncharitable to say so
—almost villanous. I think him a very ill-looking
man, and if I thought he was following us, I should
speak to the police, and then set out for my humble
home without losing an hour."

"And you don't think he is following us?" said
the young lady.

"If he is travelling to collect subscriptions he
may very well have come here about his business,
and to Penmaen Mawr, and to Chester. I don't
see why he must necessarily be following us. And
Conway, too, he would have stopped at naturally.
It does not follow at all that he is in pursuit of us
because he happens to come to the same places.

> The king himself has followed her
> When she has gone before.

We are not worth robbing, my dear, and we look
it. You must not be so easily frightened."

"Frightened! I'm not the least frightened," said the young lady, spiritedly. "I'm not what is termed a nervous young lady. You have no right to think that. But I don't believe he has any other business but tracking us from place to place. What other business on earth could he have had —getting out at Abber, for instance? I forgot to mention Abber. It is very odd, you must allow. Let us walk on." She had picked up her colour-box and her block. "Very odd that he should get out of the train wherever we stop, always about business, we are to suppose, that has no connexion with us; that he should follow us, by the same odd accident, where there is no rail, and where we can only get by a fly; that he should get always into the same quiet little inns, though, of course, he would like much better to be in noisier places, where he would meet people like himself; and that he should turn up, this evening, so near our poor little lodgings, and go by that path which brings him there. What on earth can he want in that direction?"

"Yes, I do think it's odd, my dear; and, I say, I think he does look very villanous," said the old lady.

"I don't pretend to account for it," said the girl, as they trudged on side by side; "but it is just possible that he may be a detective, who mistakes us for some people he is in pursuit of. I only know that he is spoiling my poor little holiday, and I do wish I were a man, that I might give him a good fright."

The old lady laughed, for the girl spoke threateningly, with a flash from her splendid eyes, and for a moment clenched the tiniest little fist you can fancy.

" And you think he's gone before us to Pritchard's farm-house ?" said the old lady, glancing over her shoulder in that direction, above which a mass of thundrous cloud was rising. " Dear me! how like thunder that is."

" Awfully !" said the young lady. " Stop a moment — I thought I heard distant thunder. Listen !"

They both paused, looking toward those ominous piles of cloud, black against the now fast-fading sky.

CHAPTER II.

A GUIDE.

"Hush!" said the young lady, laying her fingers on her companion's arm.

They listened for a minute or more.

"There it is!" exclaimed the girl, as a faint rumble spread slowly along, and among the mountains.

They remained silent for a minute after it had passed away.

"Yes, that certainly was thunder," said the elder lady; "and it is growing so dark; it would not do to be caught in the storm, and to meet our one-eyed persecutor, perhaps, and we have fully a mile to go still. Come, we must walk a little faster."

"I hope it will be a good thunder-storm," said

the young lady watching the sky, as they hurried on. "It frightens me more than it does you, but I think I like it better."

"You may easily do that, dear; and like our farm-house better than I do, also."

"We are frightfully uncomfortable, I agree. Let us leave it to-morrow," said the young lady.

"And where shall we go next?" inquired her companion.

"To Llanberris, if I'm to decide," said the girl. "But first we must look over the castle at Cardyllion, and there are one or two old houses I should like to sketch—only roughly."

"You are making too great a labour of your holiday: you sketch too much."

"Well, we leave to-morrow, and the day after is Sunday, and then—on Monday—my holiday ends, and my slavery begins," said the young lady, impetuously.

"You certainly do use strong language," said the elder lady, a little testily. "Why don't you try to be content? Dear me! How much nearer the thunder is!"

"It will soon be darker, and then we shall see the lightning splendidly," said the young lady.

"Don't stop, darling, let us get on. I was going to say, you must study to be content—remember your catechism. The Queen, I dare say, has things to complain of; and Farmer Pritchard's daughter, who has, as you fancy, a life of so much liberty, will tell you she is something of a slave, and can't do, by any means, quite as she likes. I only hope, dear Maud, we have money enough to bring us home."

"We can eke it out with my drawings. We shan't starve. We can have the ruins of Carnarvon Castle for breakfast, and eat Snowdon for dinner, and turn the Menai into tea. It is a comfort to know I can live by my handiwork. I don't think, cousin, I have a shilling I can call my own. If I could earn enough by my drawing to live on, I think I should prefer it to any other way of living I can imagine."

" You used to think a farmer's life the happiest on earth," said the old lady, trudging along. "There's Richard Pritchard, why not marry him ?"

" I might do worse; but there are half a dozen conclusive reasons against it. In the first place, I don't think Richard Pritchard would marry me; and, next, I know I wouldn't marry Richard Pritchard; and, thirdly, and seriously, I shall never marry at all, never, and for the reasons I have told you often; and those reasons can never change."

"We shall see," said her companion, with a

laugh and a little shake of her head. "Good Heavens!" exclaimed the old lady, as nearer thunder resounded over the landscape.

"Hush!" whispered the girl, as they both paused and listened, and when it had died away, "What a noble peal that was!" she exclaimed. And as they resumed their march she continued: "I shall never marry: and my resolution depends on my circumstances, and they, as you know, are never likely to alter—humanly speaking, they never can alter—and I have not courage enough to make myself happy; and, coward as I am, I shall break my own heart rather than break my chains. Where are we now?"

As she said this she came to a sudden halt at the edge of a deep channelled stream, whose banks just there stand steep and rugged as those of a ravine, crowned with straggling masses of thorn and briars. She gazed across and up and down the stream, which was swollen just then by mountain rains of the night before.

"Can we have missed our way?" said the elder lady.

"What on earth has become of the wooden bridge?" exclaimed the younger one.

There was still quite light enough to discern objects; and Miss Max, catching her young companion by the hand, whispered:

"Good gracious, Maud, is that the man?"

"What man?" she asked, startled.

"The blind man—the person who has been following us."

Miss Maud—for such was the young lady's name—said nothing in reply. The two ladies stood irresolute, side by side. Maud had seen the person who was approaching, once only in her life. It was two days before, as she and her cousin were getting out of their fly at the Verney Arms, in the pretty little town of Cardyllion. She was a proud young lady; it would have taken a good deal to make her avow, even to herself, the slightest interest in any such person. Nevertheless, she recognised him a good many seconds before Miss Max had discovered her mistake.

She was standing beside that elderly lady. They were both looking across the stream; the young lady furthest from the stranger had turned a little away.

There is quite light enough to see faces still, but it will not last long. The young man is very handsome, and also tall. He has been fishing, and has on a pair of those gigantic jack-boots in which fishermen delight to walk the rivers. He wears a broad-leafed hat, round which are wound his flies. A boy with his rod, net, and basket trudges behind.

The old lady speaks to him as he passes. He stops, lowers his cigar, and inclines to listen.

"I beg pardon," she says. "Can you tell me? There was—I am sure it was on this very spot— a bridge of plank across this stream, and I can't find it."

"Oh! They were taking that away to-day, as I passed by. It had grown unsafe, and the— the—— Oh, yes; the new one is to be put up in the morning."

The odd little hesitation I have recorded was caused by his seeing the young lady, on a sudden, in the midst of his sentence, and for the moment forgetting everything else. And well he might, for he had been dreaming of her for the last two days.

He dropped his cigar, became, all at once, much more deferential, and with his hat in his hand, said:

"Do you wish to cross the brook? Because if you do, I can show you to some stepping-stones about a quarter of a mile higher up, where you can get across very nicely."

"Thanks. I should be so very much obliged," said the old lady.

- The gentleman was only too happy, and having sent the boy on to the Verney Arms, talked very agreeably as he accompanied and directed their march. He had come down there for a little fishing; he knew the Verneys a little, and old Lord Verney was such a very odd man! He told them stories of him, and very amusing some of them were, and his eye always glanced to see the effect of his anecdotes upon Miss Maud. Two or three times he ventured to speak to her. The young lady did not either encourage or discourage these little experiments, and answered very easily and carelessly, and, I am bound to say, very briefly too.

In the mean time, the thunder grew nearer and more frequent, and the wild reflection of the lightning flickered on trees and fields about them.

And now they had reached the thick clump of osiers, beneath which the stepping-stones, of which they were in search, studded the stream. Only the summits of these stones were now above the water, and the light was nearly gone.

CHAPTER III.

PLAS YLWD.

"I HAVE not courage for this," said the old lady, aghast, eyeing the swift current and the uncertain footing to which, in the most deceptive possible twilight, she was invited to commit herself.

"But you know, darling, we must get across somehow," urged the girl, cruelly. "It is quite easy; don't fancy anything else."

And she stepped lightly over.

"It is all very fine with your young feet and eyes," she replied; "but for an old woman like me it is little better than the tight rope; and it would be death to me to take a roll in that river. What on earth is to be done?"

"It *is* really a great deal easier than you suppose," said the obliging young gentleman, not sorry to find an opportunity of agreeing with Miss Maud, "and I think I can make it perfectly easy if you will just take my hand as you get across. I'll walk in the stream beside you. It is quite shallow here, and these things make me absolutely impervious to the water. Pray, try. I undertake to get you across perfectly safely."

So, supporting her across with his left hand, and walking beside her, with his right ready to assist her more effectually in case of a slip or stumble, he conducted her quite safely over.

When the lady had thanked him very earnestly, and he had laughingly disclaimed all right to her acknowledgments, another difficulty suddenly struck her.

"And now, how *are* we to find our farm-house? I know the way to it perfectly from the wooden bridge; but from this, I really haven't an idea."

"I'll make it out," said the young lady, before their guide had time to speak. "I like exploring; and it can't be far—a little in this direction. Thank you very much."

The last words were to the young man, whose huge boots were pouring down rivulets on the dry dust of the little pathway on which they were standing.

"If I am not too disagreeable a guide, in this fisherman's plight," he said, glancing, with a laugh, at his boots, "nothing would please me so much as being allowed to point out the way to you. I happen to know it perfectly, and it is by no means so easy as you may suppose, particularly by this light—one can hardly tell distances, ever so near."

"Pray, don't take all that trouble," said the girl, "I can make it out quite easily."

"Nonsense, my dear Maud. You could never make it out; and besides," she added, in an under tone, "how can you tell where that blind man may turn up, that follows us, as you say? We are very much obliged to you," she said, turning to him, "and you are doing us really a great kindness. I only hope it won't be bringing you too far out of your way?"

Very pleasantly, therefore, they went on. It became darker, rapidly, and though the thunder grew louder and more frequent, and the lightning gleamed more vividly across the landscape, the storm was still distant enough to enable Maud to enjoy its sights and sounds, without a sense of danger.

The thunder-clouds are stealthily but swiftly ascending. These battlements of pandemonium, "like an exhalation," screen the sky and stars with black, and from their field of darkness leaps now

and then the throbbing blue, that leaves the eye
dazzled, and lights rock and forest, hill and ruin,
for a moment in its pale glare. Then she listens
for the rumble that swells into long and loud-
echoing reverberations. He stays his narrative,
and all stop and listen. He smiles, as from under
his long lashes he covertly watches the ecstasy of
the beautiful girl. And then they set out again ;
the old lady vowing that she can't think why she's
such a fool as to stop at such an hour, and tired to
death as she is, to listen to thunder.

Farmer Pritchard, happily for wandering Tintos
in that part of the world, is not one of those
scientific agriculturists who cut down their hedge-
rows and square their fields. Our little party has
now reached the stile which, under the shadow of
some grand old elms, admits the rustics, who frequent Richard Pritchard, to his farm-yard.

It is an old and a melancholy remark, that the
picturesque and the comfortable are hardly com-
patible. Here, however, these antagonistic principles are as nearly as possible reconciled. The
farm-yard is fenced round with hawthorns and
lime-trees, and the farm-house is a composite building, of which the quarter in which the ladies were
lodged had formed a bit of the old Tudor manor-
house of Plas Ylwd, which gave its name to the
place.

A thatched porch, with worn stone pillars and steps, fronts the hatch; and from beside this, through a wide window of small panes, a cheerful light was scattered along the rough pavement, and more faintly on the hanging foliage of the tree opposite.

"What a pretty old house!" the young fisherman exclaimed, looking up at the gables, and the lattices, and the chimneys, that rose from the deep thatch of the cobbled building.

"It may be prettier in this light, or rather darkness, than at noon," said the old lady, with a shrug, and a little laugh.

"But it really is, in any light, an extremely pretty old house," said the girl, taking up the cudgels for their habitation, "and everything is so beautifully neat. I think them such nice people."

A few heavy rain-drops had fallen sullenly as they came, and now with the suddenness of such visitations, the thunder shower, all at once, began to descend.

"Come in, come in," said the old lady, imperiously.

Very willingly the young gentleman stepped under the porch.

They all three stood there for a moment, looking out towards the point from which, hitherto, the lightning had been chiefly visible.

"Oh! But you must come in and take some tea," said the old lady, suddenly recollecting. "You *must* come in, really."

Their walk and chat, and the climbing of stiles, and the rural simplicities that surrounded, had made her feel quite intimate. He glanced covertly at the young lady, but in her face he saw neither invitation nor prohibition; so he felt at liberty to choose, and he stepped, very gladly, into the house.

As you enter the old house you find yourself in a square vestibule, if I can call by so classic a name anything so rude. Straight before you yawns an arch that spans it from wall to wall, giving admission to the large kitchen of the farm-house: at your right, under a corresponding moulded arch, opens the wide oak staircase of the manor-house, with a broad banister, on the first huge stem of which, as on a vestal altar, is placed a burnished candlestick of brass, in which burns a candle to welcome the return of old Miss Max and young Miss Maud Guendoline.

The young lady steps in with the air, though she knows it not, of a princess into her palace.

As they enter, her ear is struck by an accent, not Welsh, and a voice the tones of which have something of a cold, nasal, bleating falsetto, which is intensely disagreeable, and looking quickly through the arched entrance to the kitchen, she sees there, taking his ease in an arm-chair by the fireplace, the long-visaged man with the white eye.

He is holding forth agreeably, with a smile on his skinny lips. He gesticulates with a long hand, the nails of which are black as ebony. The steam of the saintly man's punch makes a halo round his head; and his hard cheeks are flushed with the pink that tells of inward comfort. His one effective eye addresses itself, although he is haranguing Richard Pritchard's wife, to Richard Pritchard's daughter, who is very pretty, and leans, listening to the ugly stranger, with her bare arms rolled in her apron, on the high back of one of the old-fashioned oak chairs.

CHAPTER IV.

HOW THEY ALL GOT ON.

JUST for a moment the appearance of this Cocles, domesticated under the same roof, spy, thief, whatever he might be, made the young lady wince. Her impulse was to walk straight into the kitchen, cross-examine the visitor, and call on Richard Pritchard to turn him out forthwith. But that was only for one moment; the next, she was chatting just as usual. Mrs. Pritchard, with her pretty Welsh accent, another candle, and her smile of welcome, had run out to accompany the ladies up-stairs to know their wishes, and to make any little adjustments in the room they might require.

"I lighted a bit o' fire, please 'm, the evenin' was gone rather cold, I thought."

" You did quite right, Mrs. Pritchard; you take
such good care of us; it looks so comfortable,"
said the old lady.

" I'm very glad 'm, thank you, ma'am, will you
please to have tea 'm ? "

" Yes, as quickly as possible, thanks."

And Mrs. Pritchard vanished noiselessly. The
old lady's guest was delighted with everything he
saw.

It is not a large room; square, with blackest
oak panels, burnished so that they actually flash in
the flicker of the fire, that burns under the
capacious arch of the fireplace. All the furniture,
chairs, tables, and joint stools, are of the same
black oak, waxed and polished, till it gleams and
sparkles again. These clumsy pieces of ancient
cabinet-making have probably descended, with this
wing of the old house, to its present occupiers.
The floor is also of polished oak, with a piece of
thick old carpet laid down in the middle, and the
window is covered with a rude curtain of baize.
There are two sets of shelves against the wall, on
which stand thick the brightly coloured delft
figures, cups, and candlesticks, interspersed with
mutilated specimens of old china — a kind of
ornament in which the Welsh delight, and which
makes their rooms very bright and cheerful. The
room is a picture of neatness. For a king's ran-

som you could not find dust enough in it to cover a silver penny. The young guest looks round delighted. Margaret's homely room did not seem to Faust more interesting, or more instinct with the spirit of neatness.

" Well, now you are in our farm-house, Mr.——" The old lady had got thus far, when she found herself at fault, a little awkwardly.

" My name is Marston," he said, smiling a little, but very pleasantly.

" And I think, for my part, I have seen much more uncomfortable drawing-rooms," she resumed. "I think it is a place one might grow fond of. Marston," she murmured in a reverie, and then she said to him, " I once met a Mr. Marston at——"

But here a covert glance from Maud pulled her up again.

" I certainly did meet a Mr. Marston somewhere ; but it is a long time ago," she said.

" We are to be found in three different counties," he said, laughing; " it is hard to say where we are at home."

" Aren't you afraid of those great wet boots ?" the officious old lady began.

" Oh, dear ! not the least," said he, " if you don't object to them in your drawing-room." He glanced at the young lady, so as to include her. " But the little walk up here has shaken off all the wet, and as for myself, they are a sort of diving-bells in which one can go anywhere and be as dry as on terra firma; it is the only use of them." He turned to the young lady. "Very tempting scenery about here. I dare say you have taken a long walk to-day. Some lady friends of mine, last year, over-did it very much, and were quite knocked up for some time after they left this."

"I'm a very good walker — better than my cousin," said the young lady; "and a good long walk is one of the most delightful things on earth. To see, as I have done, often, distant blue hills grow near, and reveal all their picturesque details, and a new landscape open before you, and finally to see the same hills fall into the rear, and grow as dim and blue as they were before, and to owe the transformation to your own feet, is there anything that gives one such a sense of independence? Those fine ladies who go everywhere in their carriages enjoy nothing of this, and yet, I think, it is half the pleasure of beautiful scenery. My cousin Max to-day was lecturing me on the duty of being content — I don't think that is the speech of a discontented person."

"It is a very wise speech, and perfectly true; I have experienced the same thing a thousand times myself," said Mr. Marston.

Miss Max would have had a word to say, but she

was busy hammering upon the floor with a cudgel
provided for the purpose of signalling thus for
attendance from below.

Mrs. Pritchard enters with the tea.   Is there a
cosier spectacle?   If people are disposed to be
happy, is there not an influence in the cups and
saucers, and all the rest, that makes them cheery,
and garrulous, and prone to intimacy?

It is an odd little adventure.   Outside—

> The speedy gleams the darkness swallows,
> Loud, long, and deep, the thunder bellows.

The pretty girl has drawn the curtain halfway
back, and opened a lattice in the stone-shafted
window, the air being motionless, to see the lightning better.   The rain is still rushing down
perpendicularly, and whacking the pavement below
all over.   Inside, the candles glimmer on oaken
walls three hundred years old, and a little party of
three, so oddly made acquainted, are sitting over
their homely tea, and talking as if they had known
one another as long as they could remember.

Handsome Mr. Marston is chatting in the
happiest excitement he has ever known.   The girl
can't deny, in foro conscientiæ, that his brown
features and large dark eyes, and thick soft hair,
and a certain delicacy of outline almost feminine,
accompanied with his manly and athletic figure,
present an ensemble singularly handsome.

" His face is intelligent, there is fire in his face, he looks like a hero," she admitted to herself. " But what do I know of him? He talks good-naturedly. His manners are gentle; but mamma says that young faces are all deceptive, and that character does not write itself there, or tone the voice, or impress the manner, until beauty begins to wear itself out. I know nothing about him. He seems to know some great people, but he won't talk of them to *us*. That is good-breeding, but nothing more. He seems to enjoy himself here in this homely place, and drinks his tea very happily from these odd delft cups. He brings the kettle, or hammers on the floor with that cudgel, as my cousin orders him. But what is it all? A masquerading adventure—the interest or fun of which consists in its incongruity with the spirit of his life, and its shock to his tastes. He may be cruel, selfish, disobliging, insolent, luxurious."

In this alternative she wronged him. This Charles Marston, whose letters came to him addressed the " Honourable Charles Marston," was, despite his cleverness, something of a dreamer, very much of an enthusiast, and as capable of immensurable folly, in an affair of the grand passion, as any schoolboy, in the holidays, with his first novel under his pillow.

" He can't suppose, seeing us here," thought the

girl, " that we are people such as he is accustomed
to meet. Of course he despises us. Very good,
sir. An eye for an eye," and she turned her
splendid dark eye for a moment covertly upon him,
"and a tooth for a tooth. If you despise us, I
despise you. We shall see. I shall be very direct.
I shall bring that to the test, just now. We shall
see."

Charles Marston stole beside her, and looked out,
with her, at the lightning. This is an occupation
that helps to make young people acquainted. A
pity it does not oftener occur in our climate. The
little interjections. The "oh, oh, ohs!" and
"listens," the "hushes," and "wasn't that glorious!"
"you're not afraid?" and fifty little useless but
rather tender attentions, arise naturally from the
situation. Thus an acquaintance, founded in
thunder and lightning, may, like that of Macbeth
and the witches, endure to the end of the gentleman's adventures.

Not much attended to, I admit, good Miss Max
talked on, about fifty things, and, now and then,
threw in an interjection, when an unusually loud
peal shook the walls of the old farm-house, and
was followed for a minute by a heavier cataract of
rain.

But soon, to the secret grief of Mr. Marston,
the thunder began perceptibly to grow more dis-

tant, and the lightning less vivid, and, still more terrible, the rain to abate.

The interest in the storm subsided, and Miss Maud Guendoline closed the lattice, and returned to the tea-table.

Had he ever seen in living face, in picture, in dream, anything so lovely? Such silken brown hair, such large eyes and long lashes, and beautifully red lips! Her dimples look so pretty in the oblique light and shadow, as her animated talk makes a pleasant music in his ears. He is growing more foolish than he supposes.

Miss Max, who knows nothing of him, who can't tell whether he is a nobleman or a strolling player, whether he is worth ten thousand a year, or only the clothes on his back and his enormous pair of boots, marks the symptoms of his weakness, and approves and assists with all the wise decision of a romantic old woman.

She makes an excuse of cold feet to turn about and place hers upon the fender. It is a lie, palpably, and Miss Maud is angry, and insists on talking to her, and keeping the retiring chaperon, much against her will, still in evidence.

The young man is not the least suspicious, has not an idea that good Miss Max is wittingly befriending him, but earnestly wishes that she may fall into a deep sleep in her chair.

The cruel girl, however, insists on her talking.

"I saw you talking to those American people who came into the carriage at Chester, didn't you?" said the girl.

"Yes, dear," said Miss Max, dryly; "nothing could be more uninteresting."

"I was in the waiting-room at Chester with that very party, I'm certain," said Mr. Marston. "There were two ladies, weren't there, and the man had a kind of varnished waterproof coat, and a white hat, and was very thin, and had a particularly long nose, a little crooked?"

"Yes, that is *my* friend," answered Maud. "That gentleman was good enough to take a great interest in me and my cousin. I had to inform him that my christian name is Maud and my surname Guendoline; that a friend had made me a present of my first-class ticket; that my papa has been dead for many years; and that mamma's business allows her hardly an hour to look after me; that I have not a shilling I can call my own; that I thought I could do something to earn a subsistence for myself; that I can draw a little—I can teach——"

"Where have you ever taught, dear?" threw in Miss Max, apparently in great vexation at her companion's unseasonable frankness.

"I don't say I have yet taught for money, but

I have learned something of it at the Sunday school, and I don't see why I shouldn't do it as well as mamma. Then there's my music—that ought to be worth something."

"You must be tired, I think," interrupted the old lady, a little sharply; "you have had a very long walk to-day. I think you had better go to your room."

"I have stayed, I'm afraid, a great deal too late," said Mr. Marston, who could not mistake the purport of the old lady's speech. "I'm afraid you are tired, Miss Guendoline. I'm afraid you have both been doing too much, and you'll allow me, won't you, just to call in the morning to inquire how you are?"

"It is very inhospitable," said Miss Max, relenting a little; "but we are very early people in this part of the world, and I shall be very happy to see you to-morrow, if we should happen to be at home."

He had taken his leave; he was gone. A beautiful moonlight was silvering the quaint old building and the graceful trees that surround it. The mists of night hung on the landscape, and the stars, the fabled arbiters of men's fortunes, burned brilliantly in the clear sky.

He crossed the stile, he walked along the white path, as if in a trance. He paused under a great

ash-tree, snake-bound in twisted ivy, and leaned
against its trunk, looking towards the thatched
gable of the old stone building.

"Was there ever so beautiful a creature?" he
said.   "What dignity, what refinement, what
prettiness, and what a sweet voice; what anima-
tion!   Governess, farmer's daughter, artist, be
she what she may, she is the loveliest being that
ever trod this earth !"

In this rapture—in which mingled that pain of
doubt and yearning of separation which constitutes
the anguish of such violent "fancies"—he walked
slowly to the stepping-stones, and conning over
every word she had spoken, and every look in her
changing features, he arrived at last, rather late,
at his inn, the Verney Arms, in Cardyllion.

CHAPTER V.

A SPECTRE.

The two ladies sat silent for some time after their guest had departed.

Miss Max spoke first.

" 1 don't think it is quite honest—you make me ashamed of you."

" I'm ashamed of myself. It's true; he'll think too well of me," said the girl, impetuously.

" He thinks very oddly of us both, I'm afraid," said Miss Max.

" I'm not afraid—I don't care—I dare say he does. I think you hinted that he should carry you across the stream on his back. I got out of hearing before you had done. You all but asked

D 2

him for his name, and finally turned him out in the thunder at a moment's notice."

"It does not matter what an old woman says or does, but a girl is quite different," replied Miss Max. "You need not have said one word about our ways and means."

"I shall say the same to every one that cares to hear, where I am not under constraint; and you shall keep your promise. Do let me enjoy my liberty while I may," answered the girl.

"Are you a gipsy? You are such a mixture of audacity and imposture!" said Miss Max.

"Gipsy? Yes. We are something like gipsies, you and I—our long marches and wandering lives. Imposture and audacity? I should not mind pleading guilty to that, although, when I think it over, I don't remember that I said a word that was not literally true, except my surname. I was not bound to tell that, and he would have been, I dare say, no wiser if I had. I was not bound to tell him anything. I think I have been very good."

"I dare say he is Lord Somebody," said Miss Max.

"Do you like him better for that?" asked the girl.

"You are such a radical, Maud! Well, I don't say I do. But it just guarantees that if the

man has any nice tastes, he has leisure and money
to cultivate them; and if he has kind feelings he
can indulge them, and is liberated from all those
miserable limitations that accompany poverty."

"I have made a very frank confession with one
reserve. On that point I have a right to be
secret, and you have promised secrecy. Am I
under the miserable obligation to tell my real con-
dition to every one who pleases to be curious?"

"You blush, Maud."

"I dare say I do. It is because you look at me
so steadily. I told him all I choose to tell. He
shan't think me an adventuress; no one shall. I
said enough to show I was, at least, willing to earn
an honest livelihood. I said the same to that
vulgar American, and you did not object. And
why not to him? I don't care one farthing about
him in particular. He will not pay us a visit
to-morrow, you'll find. He has dropped us, being
such as I suppose him, and we shall never see him
more. I am glad of it. Let us cease to think of
him. There's a more interesting man down-
stairs."

In her slender hand she took the stick that she
called the cudgel, and hammered on the floor.

Up came pretty Anne Pritchard, looking sleepy,
her cheeks a little pale, her large eyes a little
drowsy.

"Can I see your father, Mr. Pritchard?" asked Maud.

"He's gone to his bed, please, ma'am, an hour ago."

"Is he asleep, can you tell?"

"He goes to sleep at once, if you please, miss."

"How provoking! What shall we do?" She turned to Miss Max, and then to the girl. She said: "I saw a man, a stranger—a man with a blind eye, here, when we came in. Is he here still?"

"Yes 'm, please."

"He has a bed here, has he, and stays to-night?" asked the old lady.

"Yes 'm, please," said the girl, with a curtsy.

"What do you think? Shall we turn him out?" said Maud, turning to Miss Max.

"Oh! no, dear, don't trouble your head about him. He'll go in the morning. He's not in our way, at all," answered Miss Max.

"Well, I suppose it is not worth making a fuss about. *There* is another advantage of the visit of our friend in the boots this evening. I could not find an opportunity to tell Mr. Pritchard to turn that person out of the house," said Miss Maud, with vexation.

" Please 'm, Mr. Lizard?"

" Say it again, child, Mr. Who?" asked Miss Max.

" Mr. Lizard, please 'm. Elihu Lizard is wrote in his Bible, and he expounded this evening before he went to his bed. He's a very good man."

" Was he ever here before?" asked Miss Maud.

" No, please 'm."

" And what is he?" demanded the young lady.

" I don't know, miss. Oh, yes, please 'm, I forgot; he said he was gettin' money, please 'm, for the good of the Gospel, and he had papers and cards, 'm."

" The same story, you see," she said, turning with a little nod, and a faint smile, to her companion.

" Do let the man rest in his bed, my dear, and let us go to ours; you forget how late it is growing," said Miss Max, and yawned, and lighted her candle.

" That will do, thanks," said Maud, thoughtfully, "and will you tell Mr. Pritchard, your father, in the morning, that we wish very much to see him before we go out?"

" And let us have breakfast a little before nine, please," added Miss Max, looking at her watch, and then holding it to her ear. "Come, darling,"

she said, finding it was going, " it really is very
late, and you have a good deal, you know, to do
to-morrow."

" It is the most unpleasant thing in the world,"
said the pretty young lady, looking thoughtfully
at her companion. "There can be no question he
is following us, or one of us, you or me. Who on
earth can have sent him? Who can it be?
That odious creature! Did you ever see a more
villanous face? He is watching us, picking up
information about all our doings. What can he
want? It is certainly for no good. Who can
it be?"

" We can't find out to-night, and there is no
good in losing your sleep. Perhaps we may make
out something from old Pritchard in the morning,"
said Miss Max.

" Yes, yes, perhaps so. All I know is, it is
making me quite miserable," said the girl, and she
kissed the old lady, and went to her room. And
Miss Max, having seen that the fire was nearly
out, retired also to hers.

As neat and as quaint as their drawing-room,
was Miss Max's bedroom. But though everything
invited to rest, and Miss Max rather stiff from
her long walk, and a little drowsy and yawning,
she was one of those fidgety old ladies who take a
prodigious time to get into bed.

Nearly an hour had passed, during which she had stuck armies of pins in her pincushion, and shut and opened every drawer in her room, and walked from one table to another oftener, and made more small dispositions about her room and her bed, than I could possibly reckon, and, being now arrayed in slippers and dressing-gown, she bethought of something to be adjusted in the sitting-room, which might just as well have waited till the morning, and so she took her candle and descended the old oak stairs.

On the solid plank of that flooring, the slippered footfall of the thin old lady made no sound. The moon was high, and her cold blue light fell slanting through the window upon the floor of the little lobby. Within and without reigned utter silence; and if Miss Max had been a ghost-seeing old maid, no scene could have been better suited for the visitation of a phantom than this dissociated wing of a house more than three hundred years old.

Miss Max was now at the drawing-room door, which she opened softly and stepped in. It was neither without a tenant nor a light.

At the far corner of the table, with a candle in his hand, which he instantly blew out, she saw the slim figure and sly lean face of Elihu Lizard, his white eyeball turned towards her, and his other

eye squinting with the scowl of alarm, fiercely
across his nose, at her.

Mr. Lizard was, with the exception of his shoes
and his coat, in full costume. His stockings and
his shirt-sleeves gave him a burglarious air, which
rather heightened the shock of his ugly leer, thus
unexpectedly encountered.

He stepped back into a recess beside the chimney
almost as she entered.

For a moment she was not quite sure whether
her frequent discussions with Maud respecting
this repulsive person had not excited her fears
and fancies, so as to call up an ugly vision. Mr.
Lizard, however, seeing that the extinction of his
candle-light was without effect, Miss Max's candle
shining full upon him, stepped forward softly, and
executed his guileless smile and lowly reverence.

Miss Max had recovered her intrepidity; and
she said sharply:

"What do you mean, sir? what on earth brings
you to our private sitting-room?"

"I have took the liberty," he said, in his
quavering tones, inclining his long face aside with
a plaintive simper, nearly closing his eyelids, and
lifting one skinny hand—it was the tone and
attitude in which the good Elihu Lizard was wont
to expound, the same in which he might stand
over a cradle, and pronounce a blessing on the

little Christian in blankets, with whose purity the guileless heart of the good man sympathised— "being a-thirst and panting, so to speak, as the hart for the water-brooks, as I lay in my bed, I arose, and finding none where I looked for it, I thought it would not be grudged me even in the chambers of them that go delicately, and therefore am I found here seeking if peradventure I might find any."

Elihu Lizard, upon all occasions on which worldly men, of his rank in life, would affect the language of ceremony, glided from habit into that with which he had harangued from tables and other elevations at Greenwich Fair and similar assemblies, before he had engaged in his present peculiar occupation.

There was something celestial in the suavity of this person that positively exasperated Miss Max.

"That's all very fine. Water, indeed! There you were, over Miss Maud's and my letters and papers, in our private sitting-room, and you show, sir, that you well knew you were about something nefarious, for I saw you put out your candle— there it is, sir, in your hand. How disgusting! How dare you! And I suspect you, sir, and your impious cant; and I'll find out all about you, or I'll lose my life! How can Mr. Pritchard allow such persons into his house? I'll see him in the morning. I'll speak to the police in Cardyllion about you. I'll come to the bottom of all this. I'll consult a lawyer. I'll teach you, sir, be you who you may, you are not to follow people from place to place, and to haunt their drawing-rooms at dead of night. I'll turn the tables upon you; I'll have you pursued."

The good man turned up his effective eye, till nothing but its white was seen, and it would have been as hard to say which of the two had a pupil to it, as under which of his thimbles, if thimble-rigger he be, the pea actually lies. He smiled patiently, and bowed lowly, and with his palm raised, uttered the words, " Charity thinketh no evil."

The measure of Miss Max's indignation was full. With her brown silk handkerchief swathed tightly about her head, for she had not yet got on her nightcap; and looking somewhat like a fez, in her red cloth slippers, and white cashmere dressing-gown, that, I must allow, was rather "skimpy," showing a little more of her ankle than was quite dignified, she was a rather striking effigy of indignation. She felt that she could have hurled her candlestick at the saintly man's head, an experiment which it is as well she did not hazard, seeing that she and her adversary would have been reduced to instantaneous darkness, and might have, without intending it, encountered in the dark, while endeavouring to make their retreat. Instead, therefore, of proceeding to this extreme measure, with kindling eyes, and a stamp on the floor, she said:

"Leave this room, this moment, sir! How dare you? I shall call up Mr. Pritchard, if you presume to remain here another moment."

I dare say that Mr. Lizard had completed whatever observations he intended to make, and his reconnaissance accomplished, he did not care to remain a moment longer than was necessary under fire. He withdrew, therefore, with the smiling meekness of a Christian enduring pagan vituperation and violence.

In the morning, when, at their early breakfast, the ladies made inquiry after him, they learned that he had taken his departure more than an hour before.

"More evidence, if it were needed, of a purpose, in tracking us as he does, which won't bear the light!" exclaimed Miss Max, who was now at least as strong upon the point as the handsome girl who accompanied her. "I don't understand it. It is some object connected with *you*, most positively. Who on earth can be his employer? I confess, Maud, I'm frightened, at last."

"Do you think it can be old Mr. Tintern?"

asked the girl, after a silence, looking curiously in the face of her companion. "That old man may well wish me dead."

"It may interest, possibly, a good many people to watch you very closely," said the elder lady.

They both became thoughtful.

"You will now believe," said the young lady, with a sigh, "that the conditions of my life are not quite usual. I tell you, cousin, I have a presentiment that some misfortune impends. I suppose there is a crisis in every one's life; the astrologers used to say so. God send me safely through mine!"

"Amen, darling, if there be a crisis," said Miss Max, more gravely than she usually spoke. "But we must not croak any more. I have great confidence, under Heaven, in energy, my dear, and you were always a spirited girl. What, after all, can befal you?"

"Many things. But let us think of to-day and Cardyllion and Llanberris, and let to-morrow take care of itself. What a beautiful day!"

CHAPTER VI.

THEY MEET A FRIEND.

" WON'T you wait, and see Mr. Marston?" said Miss Max, a little later, when the young lady came down in her walking-dress.

"No, I'm going to the castle. I have planned three drawings there, and two in the town, and then we set out on our drive to Llanberris, where I shall still have daylight, perhaps, to make one or two more."

" Very industrious, upon my word! But don't you think you might afford a little time to be civil?" said Miss Max.

"I don't know what you mean."

" Mr. Marston said most pointedly, I mean, particularly, that he would call this morning, and you allowed him to suppose we should be at home."

"Did I? Well, that's past mending now," said the girl.

"And he'll come and see *no* one," said Miss Max, expanding her hands.

"He'll see the Pritchards," said Miss Maud.

"I think it extremely rude, going out so much before our usual time, as if it was just to avoid him."

"It *is* to avoid him. Put on your things and come," said the girl.

"And what reason on earth can there be?" insisted Miss Max.

"I'm not in a Marston mood this morning, that's all. Do, like a darling, put on your things and come; everything is packed, and the people here know when the fly is coming to take our boxes, and I'll walk slowly on, and you will over-take me."

So saying, she ran down-stairs, and took a very friendly leave of the Pritchard family.

She was not afraid of meeting Mr. Marston. For Anne Pritchard had told her that he had inquired at what hour the ladies usually went out to walk, and that hour was considerably later than it now was.

Miss Max overtook her.

"It's plain, we don't agree," said that lady, as if their talk had not been suspended for a moment. "I like that young man extremely, and I do think that it is rather marked, our leaving so unnecessarily early. I hate rudeness—*wanton* rudeness."

The girl smiled pleasantly on her companion.

"Why do you like him?" she said.

"Because I think him so extremely nice. I thought him so polite, and there was so much deference and delicacy."

"I'm afraid I've interrupted a very interesting acquaintance," said Miss Maud, laughing.

"But tell me why you have changed your mind, for you did seem to like him?" said Miss Max.

"Well, don't you think he appeared a little more assured of his good reception than he would have been if he had thought us persons of his own rank—I mean two great ladies such as he is in the habit of seeing; such as the people he knows? People like the Marstons—if he *is* one of them, as you suppose—make acquaintance with persons dressed in serge, like us, merely for amusement. Their affected deference seems to me insulting; it is an amusement I shan't afford him. From this point of view we can study human nature, because we can feel its meanness."

"You are a morbid creature," said Miss Max.

"I am trying to discover truth. I am trying to comprehend character," said the girl.

"And making yourself a cynic as fast as you can," said the old lady.

"It matters little what I am. We shan't see to-day a person so reckless of the future, a person with so little hope, a person who sees so little to live for, as I; or one who is so willing to die."

"Look round, my dear, and open your eyes. You know nothing of life or of God's providence," said Miss Max. "I have no patience with you."

"You were born free," said the girl, more gently than before, "I, a slave. Yes, don't smile; I call things by their names. You walk in the light, and I in darkness. The people who surround you, be they what they may, are at all events what they seem. When I look round, do I see images of candour? No; shadows dark and cold. I can trust no one—assassins in masquerade."

"Every one," said Miss Max, "has to encounter deceit and hypocrisy in this world."

"It won't do; no, it won't do. You know very well that the cases are quite different," said the girl. "I have no one to care for me, and many that wish me dead; and, except you, I can trust no one."

"Well, marry, and trust your husband."

"I've too often told you I never shall, *never*. I

need say so no more. How well the castle looks! I suppose it is from the rain last night; how beautifully the tints of the stone have come out!"

It was a brilliant, sunny morning. The grey walls, with patches of dull red and yellow stones, and cumbrous folds of ivy, looked their best, and tower, and arch, and battlement looked, in the soft summer air, all that the heart of an artist could desire.

Going to and fro from point to point, sometimes beyond the dry castle moat, sometimes within its grass-grown court, Miss Maud sketched industriously for some hours, and from her little tin colour-box threw in her tints with a bold and delicate brush, while Miss Max, seated beside her, read her book—for she loved a novel—and, through her spectacles, with glowing eyes, accompanied the heroine through her flirtations and agonies, to her final meeting with the man of her choice, at the steps of the altar.

For a little time, now and then, pretty Miss Maud would lower her pencil, and rest her eye and hand, and think, looking vaguely on the ruins, in a sad reverie.

By this time Mr. Marston had, it was to be supposed, made his visit at the old farm-house, had sustained his disappointment, and perhaps got over it, and was, possibly, consoling himself in his jack-boots, with his rod, in the channel of some distant trout-stream.

I can't say whether her thoughts ever wandered to this Mr. Marston, who was so agreeable and good-looking. But I fancy she did not think of him quite so hardly as she spoke. Whatever her thoughts were, her looks, at least, were sad.

"Whose epitaph are you writing, my dear?" inquired Miss Max, who had lowered her book, and, glancing over her spectacles, observed the absent and melancholy looks of the girl.

"My own," said she, with a little laugh. "But we have talked enough about that—I mean my life—and I suppose a good epitaph should sum that up. What do you think of these?" and she dropped her sketches on her cousin's lap. "If I finish them as well as I have begun, they will be worth three shillings each, I dare say."

"Yes; dear me! It is very good indeed. And this—how very pretty!" and so on, as she turned them over.

"But not one among them will ever be half so good as our dear old farm-house, that was so comfortable and so *uncomfortable*—so nearly intolerable, and yet so delightful; such a pleasant adventure to remember. I am very glad to have it, for we shall never see its face again."

At these words, unexpectedly, Miss Max rose,

and showed by her countenance that she saw some one approaching whom she was glad to greet. Her young companion turned also, and saw Mr. Marston already very near.

He was so delighted to see them. He had been to the old house, and was so disappointed; and the people there could not tell where they had gone. He had hoped they had changed their minds about leaving Cardyllion so soon. He had intended going to Llanberris that day, but some of his people were coming to Cardyllion. He had received orders from home to engage rooms at the Verney Arms for them, and must stay that day. It was too bad. Of course he was very glad to see them; but he might just as well have seen them in a week. Were they (Miss Max and her companion) going to stay any time at Llanberris?

"No. They would leave it in the morning."

"And continue their tour? Where?"

"Nowhere," said Miss Max. "We go home then."

He looked as if he would have given worlds to ask them where that home was.

"My cousin returns to *her* home, and I to mine," said the girl, gravely. "We are very lucky in our last day; it would have been so provoking to lose it."

"She has made ever so many drawings to-day,"

said Miss Max; "and they are really so very good,
I must show them to you."

"There is not time," said the girl to her cousin.
"It is a long drive to Llanberris; it is time we
were at the Verney Arms. We must ask after
our boxes, and order a carriage. It is later than I
fancied," she said, turning to Mr. Marston; "how
time runs away when one is really working."

"Or really happy," said the young man.

He walked with them down Castle-street to the
Verney Arms, talking with them like an old friend
all the way.

They all went together into the room to which
the waiter showed them. And Miss Max, who
had the little portfolio in her charge, said:

"Now, Maud, we must show Mr. Marston to-
day's drawings."

And very glad he was of that privilege.

Then she showed him the sketch of the old
farm-house.

"Oh! How pretty! What a sweet thing that
is! What a beautiful drawing it makes!"

And so he descanted on it in a rapture.

"There is a place here where they do photo-
graphs; and I am going to have that old house
taken," he said to the young lady, as Miss Max
was giving some orders at the door: "I like it

better than anything else about here. I feel so grateful to it."

Miss Max was back again in a moment.

"Well, I do think they *are* very pretty indeed," she said. "We'll take the portfolio inside, dear. I'll take charge of it," she said to Maud. "And I hope none of our boxes were forgotten. I must count them. Five altogether."

And she ran out again upon this errand; and Mr. Marston resumed:

"I shall never forget that thunder-storm, nor that pretty little room, nor my good fortune in being able to guide you home. I shall never forget yesterday evening, the most delightful evening I ever passed in my life."

He was speaking in a very low tone.

Miss Maud looked embarrassed, almost vexed, and a beautiful colour flushed her cheeks, and gave a fire to her dark eyes.

Mr. Marston felt instinctively that he had been going a little too fast.

"Good Heavens!" he thought, "what a fool I am! She looked almost angry. What business had I to talk so?"

There was a little silence.

"It is a misfortune, I believe, being too honest," he said at length.

"A great one, but there are others greater," said the girl, with eyes still vexed and fiery.

"What do you mean?"

"I mean being ever so little *dis*honest, and ever so little insolent. I hope I'm not that, at least to people I suppose to be my inferiors, though I may plead guilty to the lesser fault; perhaps I *am* too honest."

Very proud, at least, she looked at that moment, and very completely "floored" looked poor Mr. Marston.

I don't know what he might have said, or how much worse he might have made matters in the passionate effort to extricate himself, if Miss Max had not happened at that moment to return.

That he could be suspected of presuming upon her supposed position, to treat her with less deference than the greatest lady in the land, was a danger he had never dreamed of; he, who felt, as he spoke, as if he could have fallen on his knees before her. How monstrous! what degradation, what torture!

"Everything is ready, and the carriage at the door, my dear; and all our boxes quite right," said Miss Max, in a fuss.

Mr. Marston came down to put the ladies into their carriage; and while Miss Max was saying a word from one carriage window, he leaned for a moment at the other, and said:

"I'm so shocked and pained to think I have been so mistaken. I implore of you to believe that I am incapable of a thought that could offend you, and that you leave me very miserable."

The cheery voice of Miss Max, unconscious of her cruelty, interrupted him with a word or two of farewell, and the carriage drove off, leaving him not less melancholy than he had described himself.

CHAPTER VII.

FLIGHT.

THE old lady looked from the window as they drove on, watching the changes of the landscape. The girl, on the contrary, leaned back in her place, and seemed disturbed and thoughtful.

After a silence of nearly ten minutes, Miss Max, having had, I suppose, for the time, enough of the picturesque, remarked suddenly:

"Mr. Marston is, as I suspected, Lord War-hampton's son. His eldest, I believe his only living son. The people at the Verney Arms told me he had actually ordered horses for Llanberris, intending to go there to-day, when his plans were upset by his father's letter. Of course we know perfectly why he wished to go there to-day. I mentioned last night that we intended visiting it this afternoon, and he really did look so miserable as we took our leave just now."

"The fool! What right has he to follow us to Llanberris?" asked the girl.

"Why, of course, he has a right to go to Llanberris if he likes it, without asking either you or me," said Miss Max.

"He has just the same right, I admit, that Mr. Elihu Lizard has."

"Oh! come, you mustn't compare them," said Miss Max. "I should have been very glad to see Mr. Marston there, and so should you; he is very agreeable, and never could be the least in one's way; he's so good-natured and considerate, and would see in a moment if he was de trop. And it is all very fine talking independence; but every one knows there are fifty things we can't do so well for ourselves, and he might have been very useful in our walks."

"Carrying us over rivers in his jack-boots?"

"He never did carry me over any river, if you mean that," said Miss Max, a little testily, "or anywhere else. But it is very well I had his arm to lean upon, over those stepping-stones, or I don't think we should have got home last night."

"I dare say he thinks his title irresistible, and that the untitled and poor are made for his amuse-

ment. It is a selfish, cruel world. You ought to
know it better than I; you have been longer in it;
and yet, by a kind of sad inspiration, I know it,
I'm sure, ever so much better than you do."

"Wise-head!" said the old lady with a smile,
and a little shake of her bonnet.

The young lady looked out, and in a little time
took up a volume of Miss Max's nearly finished
novel, and read listlessly. She was by no means
in those high spirits that had hitherto accompanied
every change of scene in their little excursion.
Miss Max remarked this subsidence, thought even
that she detected the evidence of positive fatigue
and melancholy; but the wary lady made no
remark. It was better to let this little cloud dis-
sipate itself.

In a lonely part of the road a horse dropped a
shoe, and brought them to a walk, till they had
reached the next smithy. The delay made their
arrival late. The sun was in the west when they
gained their first view of that beautiful and melancholy lake lying in the lap of its lonely glen.
They drew up near the ruined tower that caught
the slanting light from the west, under the purple
shadow of the hill.

As they stopped the carriage here and got out,
they were just in time to see a man descend from
the box beside the driver.

They were both so astounded that neither could find a word for some seconds. It was Mr. Elihu Lizard, who had enjoyed all the way a seat on their driver's box, and who now got down, put his bundle on the end of his stick, which he carried over his shoulder, and with a " Heaven bless you, friend," to the whip on the box, smiled defiantly over his shoulder at the ladies, and marched onward toward the little inn at the right of the glen.

" Well!" exclaimed Miss Max, when she had recovered breath. " Certainly ! Did you ever hear or see anything like that ? Where did you take up that person, pray ?"

Miss Max looked indignantly up at the fat, dull cheeks of the Welshman on the box, and pointed with her parasol at the retreating expounder. That gentleman, glancing back from time to time, was taken with a fit of coughing, or of laughter, it was difficult to say which at that distance, as he pursued his march, with the intention of refreshing himself with a mug of beer in the picturesque little inn.

" Call that man ! You had no business taking any one upon the carriage we had hired, without our leave," said Miss Max. " Call him—make him come back, or you shall drive us after him. I will speak to him."

The driver shouted. Mr. Lizard waved his hand.

"I'm certain he is laughing—insolent hypo-crite!" exclaimed Miss Max, transported with in-dignation. "I'll drive after him, I will overtake him."

They got into the carriage, overtook Elihu Lizard, and stepped down about a dozen yards before him.

"So, sir, you persist in following us!" exclaimed the old lady.

"To me," he replied, in a long-drawn, bleating falsetto, as he stood in his accustomed pose, with his hand a little raised, his eyes nearly closed, and a celestial simper playing upon his conceited and sinister features, "to me it would appear, neverthe-less, honourable lady, that it is you, asking your parding, that is a-following of me; I am following, not you, nor any other poor, weak, sinful, erring mortal, but my humble calling, which I hope it is not sich as will be disdained from the hand of a poor weak, miserable creature, nor yet that I shall be esteemed altogether an unprofitable servant."

"I don't want to hear your cant, sir; if you had the least regard for truth, you would admit frankly that you have been following me and my friend the whole of the way from Chester, stopping wherever we stopped, and pursuing wherever we went. I have seen you everywhere, and if there was a policeman here, I should have you arrested;

rely on it, I shall meet you somewhere, where I can have your conduct inquired into, and your cowardly persecution punished."

"I have come to this land of Wales, honourable lady, and even to this place, which it is called Llanberris, holding myself subject and obedient unto the powers that be, and fearing no one, insomuch as I am upon my lawful business, with your parding for so saying, not with a concealed character, nor yet with a forged name, nor in anywise under false pretences; but walking in my own humble way, and being that, and only that, which humbly and simply I pretend to be."

The good man, with eyes nearly closed, between the lids of which a glitter was just perceptible, betraying his vigilance, delivered these words in his accustomed singsong, but with an impertinent significance that called a beautiful rush of crimson to the younger lady's cheeks.

"Your name is nothing to us, sir. We are not likely to know it," said the young lady, supporting Miss Max with a little effort. "We shall find that out in good time, perhaps. We shall make it out when we want it."

"You shall have it when you please, honourable lady; the humble and erring sinner who speaks to you is one who walks in the light, which he seeks not, as too many do, and have done, ay, and are doing at this present time, to walk as it were in a lie, and give themselves out for that which they are not. No, he is not one of those who loveth a lie, nor yet who is filled with guile, and he is not ashamed, neither afraid, to tell his name whithersoever he goeth, neither is he the heaviness of his mother; no, nor yet forsaketh he the law of his mother."

The same brilliant blush tinged the girl's cheeks: she looked hard and angrily at the man, and his simper waxed more than ever provoking as he saw these signs of confusion.

"I believe I did wrong to speak to you here, where there are no police," said Miss Max. "I ought to have known that it could only supply new opportunity to your impertinence. I shall find out, however, when I meet you next, as I have told you, whether we are longer to be exposed to this kind of cowardly annoyance."

Miss Max and her young companion turned away. The one-eyed Christian, apostle, detective, whatever he was, indulged silently in that meanest of all laughs, the laugh which, in cold blood, chuckles over insult, as with a little hitch of his shoulder, on which rested his stick and bundle, he got under way again toward the little inn, a couple of hundred yards on.

The driver took his horses up to the inn.

"Well," said Miss Max, a little disconcerted, "I could have told you that before. I thought him a very impertinent person, and just the kind of man who would be as insolent as he pleased to two ladies, alone as we are; but very civil if a gentleman were by with a stick in his hand."

"I don't mean to make any drawings here. I've changed my mind," said Maud. "I'm longing to be at Wybourne again. Suppose, instead of staying here, we go to-night?"

"Very good, dear. To say truth, I'm not comfortable with the idea of that man's being here to watch us. Come, Maud, you must not look so sad. We have all to-morrow at Wybourne, before we part, and let us enjoy, as you say, our holiday."

"Yes, on Monday we part. Don't mention it again. It is bad enough when it comes. Then the scene changes. I'll think of it no more to-day. I'll forget it. Let us walk a little further up the glen, and see all we can, in an hour."

So with altered plans the hour was passed; and at the approach of sunset they met the train at Bangor.

A fog was spreading up the Menai as the train started. To the girl it seemed prophetic of her own future of gloom and uncertainty.

Other people had changed their plans that evening. A letter had reached Mr. Marston, unluckiest of mortals, only two hours after the ladies had left Cardyllion for Llanberris, countermanding all his arrangements for his father, Lord Warhampton.

Instantly that impetuous young man had got horses, and pursued to Llanberris, but only to find that those whom he had followed had taken wing. As he looked from the uplands along the long level sweep that follows the base of the noble range of mountains, by which the line of rails stretches away until it rounds the foot of a mighty headland at the right, he saw, with distraction, the train gliding away along the level, submerging itself, at last, in the fog that flooded the valley like a golden lake.

His only clue was one of the papers, condemned as illegible, which Miss Max had hastily written for their boxes.

"Miss M. Guendoline," was written on it, with the name of some place, it was to be supposed— but, oh, torture!—the clumsy hoof of the driver, thick with mud, had stamped this inestimable record into utter illegibility. Vià Chester was still traceable, also England in the corner. The rest was undecipherable. The wretch seemed to have jumped upon it. The very paper was demolished.

The gravel from the Vandal's heel was punched through it.

In the little inn where he had heard tidings of two ladies, with a carriage such as he described, he had picked up this precious, but torturing bit of paper.

CHAPTER VIII.

WYBOURNE CHURCHYARD.

IN a golden mist he lost her; but he does not despair. Mr. Marston pursues. Has he any very clear idea why?

If he had overtaken the ladies, as he expected, at Llanberris, would he have ventured, of his own mere motion, to accompany them on their after-journey? Certainly not. What, then, is the meaning of this pursuit? What does he mean to do or say?

He has no plan. He has no set speech or clear idea to deliver. He is in a state of utter confusion. He only knows that see her once more he must—that he can't endure the thought of letting her go, thus, for ever from his sight; she is never for a moment out of his head.

I don't know what his grave and experienced servant thought of their mysterious whirl to Chester by the night mail. He did not refer it, I dare say, to anything very wise or good. But the relation of man and master is, happily, military, and the servant's conscience is acquitted when he has obeyed his orders.

The fog has melted into clearest air, and the beautiful moon is shining.

What a world of romance, and love, and beauty he thinks it, as he looks out of the open window on the trees and mountains that sail by in that fairy light.

The distance is shortening. Everything near and far is good of its kind. Everything is interesting. It is like the ecstasy of the opium-eater. Never were such stars, and hedges, and ditches. What an exquisite little church, and tombstones! Requiescat in pace! What a beautiful ash-tree! Heaven bless it! How picturesque that horse's head, poking out through the hole in the wall with the ivy over it! And those pigs, lying flat on the manure-heap, jolly, odd creatures! How delightfully funny they are! And even when he draws his head in, and leans back for a moment in his place, he thinks there is something so kindly and

jolly about that fat old fellow with the travelling-
cap and the rugs, who snores with his chin on his
chest—a stock-broker, perhaps.   What heads and
ledgers!—wonderful fellows!   The valves and
channels through which flows into its myriad
receptacles the incredible and restless wealth of
Britain.   Or, perhaps, a merchant, princely, bene-
volent.   Well that we have such a body, the glory
of England!

The fat gentleman utters a snort, wakes up,
looks at his watch, and produces a tin sandwich-
box.

That thin elderly lady in black, that sits at the
left of the fat gentleman, who is champing his
sandwiches, does not see things, with her sunken
eyes, as Mr. Marston sees them.   She is gliding
on to her only darling at school, who lies in the
sick-house in scarlatina.

They are now but half an hour from Chester.
Mr. Marston is again looking out of the window as
they draw near.

"Maud Guendoline," he is repeating again.
"Guendoline—an old surname, but so beautiful.
Foreign, is it?   I never heard it before.   When
we get into Chester I'll have the Army List, and
the London Directory, and every list of names
they can make me out.   It may help me.   Who
knows?"

They are in Chester. Oh, that it were not so big a place! His servant is looking after his luggage. He is in the ticket-office, making futile inquiries after "an old lady, Miss Max, who left Bangor for Chester that very evening, and forgot something of importance, and I would gladly pay any one a reward who could give me a clue to find her by. I am sure only that she was to go viâ Chester.

No; they could tell him nothing. But if it was viâ Chester, she was going on by one of the branches. The clerk who might have written the new labels for her luggage was not on duty till to-morrow afternoon, having leave till two. "He's very sharp; if 'twas he did it—Max is a queer name—he'll be like to remember it; that is, he may."

Here was hope, but hope deferred. The people at Llanberris had told him that the label which he had picked up was the only one on which the name of the place was written, on which account it was removed, and all the rest were addressed simply "Chester." He has nothing for it but patience.

There is a pretty little town called Wybourne, not very far from a hundred miles away. Next evening, the church-bell, ringing the rustics to evening service, has sounded its sweet note over the chimneys of the town, through hedge-rows and bosky hollows, over slope and level sward, and Mr. Marston, with the gritty dust of the railway still on his hat, has tapped in the High-street at the post-office wooden window-pane, and converses with grave and plaintive Mrs. Fisher.

"Can you tell me if a lady named Miss Guendoline lives anywhere near this?" he inquires.

"Guendoline? No, sir. But there's Mr. and Mrs. Gwyn, please, that lives down the street near the Good Woman."

"No, thanks; that's not it. Miss Maud Guendoline."

Mrs. Fisher put an unheard question to an invisible interlocutor in the interior, and made answer: "No, sir; please there's no such person."

"I beg pardon; but just one word more. Does a lady named Max—a Miss Max—live anywhere near this place?"

"Miss Max? I think not, sir."

"You're not quite sure, I think?" says he, brightening, as he leans on the little shelf outside the window; and if his head would have fitted through the open pane, he would, I think, in his eagerness, have popped it into Mrs. Fisher's front parlour.

Again Mrs. Fisher consulted the inaudible oracle.

"No, sir; we don't receive no letters here for no person of that name," she replied.

The disappointment in the young man's handsome face touched Mrs. Fisher's gentle heart.

"I'm very sorry, indeed, sir. I wish very much we could a' gave you any information," she says, through the official aperture.

"Thank you . very much," he answers, desolately. "Is there any other post-office near? Do the people send a good way to you—about what distance round?"

"Well, the furthest, I think, will be Mr. Wyke's, of Wykhampton, about four miles."

"Is there any name at all like Max, Miss Max, an old lady? I should be so extremely—I can't tell you—so very grateful." He pleads, in his extremity, "Do, do, pray ask."

She turned and consulted the unknown once more.

"There is no one—that is, no surname—here, sir, at all like Max. There's an old lady lives near here, but it can't be her. She's Miss Maximilla Medwyn."

"Maximilla? Is she an old lady?"

"Yes sir."

" Thin ?"

" She is, sir." And Mrs. Fisher begins to wonder at the ardour of his inquiries, and to look at him very curiously.

" Has she been from home lately?"

" I think she was." (Here she again consults her unseen adviser.) " Yes, sir; she returned only last night."

" And where does she live, pray? In the town here—near this ?" he pursues.

" In the Hermitage, please, sir; any one you meet will show it you. It is just at the end of the town. But she'll be in church at present."

" And how soon do you think it will be over—how soon will the people be coming out ?"

" In about half an hour, sir."

And so, with many acknowledgments on his part, and no little surprise and conjecture on that of sedate Mrs. Fisher, who wondered what could have fired this young gentleman so about old Miss Medwyn, the conference ends, and in ten minutes more, in a somewhat less dusty state, he presents himself at the open gate of the church-yard, and reconnoitres.

Over the graves in faint gusts peals the swell of the organ, and the sound of voices, sweetly and sadly, like psalmody from another world. He looks up to the gilded hand of the clock in the ivied tower, and conjectures that this must be the holy song that precedes the sermon. Devoutly he wishes the pulpit orator a quick deliverance.

He, on the whole, wisely resolves against going into the church, and, being provided with a seat, perhaps in some corner of difficult egress, whence, if he should see the objects of his pursuit, he might not be able to make his way out in time without a fuss.

At length, with a flutter at his heart, he sees the hats and bonnets begin to emerge from the porch. Taking his stand beside the gate, he watches. Not a single Christian in female garb escapes him. He sees the whole congregation pour itself out, and waits till the very dregs and sediment drop forth. Those who pray, in formâ pauperis, and draw a weekly dividend out of the poors' box : old Mrs. Milders, with the enormous black straw bonnet, and the shaking head and hand ; Bill Hopkins, lame of a leg, who skips slowly down on a crutch ; and Tom Buzzard, blind of both eyes, a pock-marked object of benevolence, with his chin high in the air, and a long cudgel in his hand, with which he taps the curbstone, and now and then the leg of a passenger who walks the street forgetful of the blind.

The clerk comes forth demurely with a black bag, such as lawyers carry their briefs in. There

is no good, Mr. Marston thinks, in waiting for the
sexton.

He joins the clerk, compliments him on his
church and organ, asks whether Miss Maximilla
Medwyn was in church—(yes, she was)—and
where the house called the Hermitage is to be
found.

"You may go by the road, sir," said the clerk,
"or by the path, which you'll find it shorter. Take
the first stile to your right, when you turn the
corner."

Alas! what is the meaning of this walk to the
Hermitage? Miss Medwyn was in church; and
could he not swear that, in the review just ended,
he had seen distinctly every female face and figure
in the congregation as it "marched past?" His
Miss Max was assuredly not among them; and she
and Miss Medwyn, therefore, were utterly distinct
old women—ah, well-a-day!

He crosses the stile. The path traverses a
narrow strip of meadow, the air is odorous with
little dishevelled cocks of hay, mown only the day
before; the spot cloistered in by very old and high
hawthorn hedges, is silent with a monastic melancholy.

He sighs more pleasantly as he enters this fra-
grant solitude; beyond the stile at the other side, is

the gloom of tall old trees. He is leaving the world behind him.

Butterflies are hovering up and down, along the hedge, at the sunny side of the field. A bee booms by as he stands on the second stile; it is the only sound he hears except the faint chirp of the grasshopper. He descends upon that pleasant dark-green grass that grows in shade.

Here is another field, long and narrow, silent and more gloomy than the first. Up the steep, a giant double row of lime-trees stretches, marking the line of the avenue, now carpeted over with thick grass, of the old manor-house of Wybourne, some walls and stone-shafted windows of which, laden with ivy, and canopied by ancient trees, crown the summit. The western sun throws long dim shadows down the slope. A thick underwood straggles among the trunks of the lordly timber, and here and there a gap leaves space, in which these patriarchal trees shake their branches free, and spread a wider shadow.

In this conventual obscurity, scarcely fifty steps up the gentle slope, he sees Miss Maud, Maud Guendoline, or whatever else her name may be, standing in her homely dress. She is looking toward him, no doubt recognises him, although she makes no sign. His heart thumps wildly once or

twice. He is all right again in a moment. He
quickens his pace. He is near enough to see her
features distinctly. She looks a little grave, he
thinks, as he raises his hat.

Here is a tall fellow, great in a town-and-gown
row, full of pluck, cool as marble in danger, very
much unnerved at this moment, and awfully afraid
of this beautiful and slender girl.

CHAPTER IX.

THE YOUNG LADY SPEAKS.

"I'm so glad, I'm so charmed—how extremely lucky I am! I had not the least hope of this. And you have made your journey quite safely?"

As he makes this little confession and inquiry, his brown handsome face and large eyes are radiant with happiness.

"Safely! oh, yes, my cousin and I are old travellers, and we never lose our way or our luggage. I am waiting here for her; she is paying a visit to—I really forget his name, farmer something or other, an old friend of hers, down there; you can see the smoke of his chimney over the hedge," said the young lady, indicating the direction.

"And you're not fatigued?"

"Oh, no! thanks."

"And Miss Max quite well, I hope?" he adds, recollecting her right to an inquiry.

"Miss Max is very well, thanks," said the young lady.

Had she blushed when she saw him? Was there not a gentle subsidence in the brilliant tint with which she met him? He thought her looking more beautiful than ever.

"I dare say you are glad to find yourself at home again?" says he, not knowing what exactly to say next.

She glanced at him as if she suspected a purpose in his question.

"Some people have no place they can call a home, and some who have are not glad to find themselves there. I'm not at home, and I'm not sorry," she said, ever so little bitterly.

"There is a great deal of melancholy in that," he said, in a lower tone, as if he would have been very glad to be permitted to sympathise. "Away from home, and yet no wish to return. Isn't it a little cruel, too?"

"Melancholy or cruel, it happily concerns no one but myself," she said, a little haughtily.

"Everything that can possibly concern your

happiness concerns me," said the young man, audaciously.

She looked for a moment offended and even angry, but " a change came o'er the spirit of her dream," and she smiled as if a little amused.

"You seem, Mr. Marston, to give away your sympathy on very easy terms—you must have mistaken what I said. It was no confidence. It was spoken, as people in masks tell their secrets, and further because I don't care if all the world knew it. How can you tell that I either desire or deserve pity; yours, or any other person's? You know absolutely nothing of me."

"I'm too impetuous; it is one of my many faults. Other fellows, wiser men, get on a thousand times better, and I have laid myself open to your reproof, and—and—disdain, by my presumption, by my daring to speak exactly as I feel. It is partly this, that the last three days—they say that happy days seem very short—I don't know how it is, I suppose I'm different from every one else; but that day, yesterday, and to-day, seem to me like three weeks; I feel as if I had known you ever so long——"

"And yet you know nothing about me, not even my name," said the young lady, smiling on the grass near her pretty foot, and poking at a daisy with the tip of her parasol, and making its little head nod this way and that.

"I do know your name—I beg pardon, but I do; I heard Miss Max call you Maud, and I learned quite accidentally your second name yesterday."

Miss Maud looks at him from under her dark lashes suddenly. Her smile has vanished now; she looks down again; and now it returns darkly.

"I do upon my honour, I learned it at Llanberris yesterday," he repeated.

"Oh! then you *did* go to Llanberris; and you did not disdain to cross-examine the people about us, and to try to make out that which you supposed we did not wish to disclose?"

"You are very severe," he began, a good deal abashed.

"I'm very merciful, on the contrary," she said, bitterly; "if I were not—but no matter I think I can conjecture who was your informant. You made the acquaintance of a person blind of one eye, who is a detective, or a spy, or a villain of some sort, and you pumped him. Somehow, I did not think before that a gentleman was quite capable of that sort of thing."

"But, I give you my honour, I did nothing of the kind." He pleads earnestly. "I saw no such person, I do assure you."

"You shall answer my questions, then," she said, as imperiously as a spoiled child; "and, first, will you speak candidly? Will you be upon honour, in no one particular, wilfully to deceive me?"

"You are the last person on earth I should deceive, upon any subject, Miss Guendoline—I hope you believe me."

"Well, why did you go to Llanberris?"

"I had hopes," he answered with a little embarrassment, "of overtaking you and Miss Max—and I—I hoped, also, that perhaps you would permit me to join in your walk—that was my only reason."

"Now, tell me my name?" said the young lady, suddenly changing her line of examination.

"Your name is, I believe—I think, you are, Miss Maud Guendoline," he answered.

She smiled again darkly at the daisy she was busy tapping on the head.

"Miss Maud Guendoline," she repeated, very low; and she laughed a little to herself.

"Maud and Guendoline are two christian names," she said. "Do you really believe that I have no surname; or perhaps you believe that either of these is my surname? I need not have told you, but I do, that neither of these is the

least like it.   And now, why have you come here?
Have you any real business here?"

"You are a very cruel inquisitor," he says, with
a very real wince.   "Is there any place where an
idle man may *not* find himself, without well knowing why?   Is your question quite fair?"

"Is your answer quite frank?   Do you quite
remember your promise?   If we are not to part
this moment, you must answer without eva-
sion."

This young lady, in serge, spoke as haughtily as
if she were a princess in a fairy-tale.

"Well, as you command me, I will, I will,
indeed.   I—I believe I came here, very much—
entirely, indeed, from the same motive that led me
to Llanberris.   I could not help it, I couldn't,
upon my honour!   I hope you are not very
angry."

It is not usual to be constrained to speak, in
matters of this kind, the literal truth; and I question if the young man was ever so much embarrassed in all his days.

"Mr. Marston," she said, very quietly, he
fancied a little sadly, "you are, I happen to know,
a person of some rank, and likely to succeed to
estates, and a title—don't answer; I *know* this to
be so, and I mention it only by way of preface.

Now, suppose I pull off my glove, and show you a seamstress's finger, dotted all over with the needle's point; suppose I fill in what I call my holiday by hard work with my pencil and colour-box; suppose, beside all this, I have troubles enough to break the spirits of the three merriest people you know; and suppose that I have reasons for preventing any one, but Miss Max, from knowing where I am, or suspecting who I am, don't you think there is enough in my case to make you a little ashamed of having pried and followed as you are doing?"

"You wrong me—oh, *indeed*, you wrong me! You won't say that; I did, perhaps, wrong. I may have been impertinent; but the meanness of prying, you *won't* think it! All I wanted was to learn where you had gone: my crime is in following you. I did not intend that you should think I had followed. I hoped it might appear like accident. If you knew how I dread your contempt, and how I respect you, and how your reproof pains me, I am sure you would think differently, and forgive me."

I don't think there could have been more deference in his face and tones if he had been pleading before an empress.

The young lady's dark eyes for a moment

looked full at him, and again down upon the little daisy at her foot; and she drew some odd little circles round it as she looked, and I think there was ever so slight a brightening of her colour while the end of her parasol made these tiny diagrams.

If a girl be only beautiful enough, and her beauty of the refined type, it is totally impossible, be her position, her dress, her associates what they may, to connect the idea of vulgarity with her. There is nothing she does or means that is not elegant. Be she what she may, and you the most conceited dog on earth, there is a superiority in her of which your inward nature is conscious, and if you see her winnowing barley, as honest Don Quixote said of his mistress, the grains are undoubtedly pearls.

Mr. Marston, in the influence of this beauty, was growing more and more wild and maudlin every moment.

"The world's all wrong," he said, vehemently; "it is always the best and the noblest that suffer most; and you say you have troubles, and you don't disdain to work, and are not ashamed of it; and I admired and respected you before, and I've learned to honour you to-day. You talk of rank: of course, there are things in its favour—some things; but there are ever so many more against it. I have little to boast of even in that, and I never was so happy as when I knew nothing about it. People are always happy, I am sure, in proportion as the idea of it fades from their minds. There is but one thing worth living for—and, oh, Heaven, how I wish I were worthy of you!"

"Now, Mr. Marston, you are talking like a madman. There must be no more of that," she said, in earnest.

"I spoke the truth, straight from my heart. I believe that is always madness."

"I like truth pretty well. I speak it more boldly than most girls, I believe. But I quite agree with you, whenever one is noble one is inevitably foolish. I'm not very old, but I have heard a good deal of romantic talk in my time, as every girl does, and I despise it. It doesn't even embarrass me. If we are to talk till my cousin, Miss Max, comes back, do let it be reasonably; I shall tire of it instantly on any other terms."

"When you told me to speak truth, just now, you did not think so," says he, a little bitterly.

"Why can't you speak to me, for a few minutes, as you would to a friend? You talked just now about rank as if it should count for nothing. I

don't agree with you. It is no illusion, but a
cruelly hard fact. If I were the sort of girl who
could like any one—I mean, make a fool of myself
and fall in love—that person must be exactly of
my own rank, neither above nor below it. The
man who stoops is always sorry for it too late; and
if he is like me, he would always think he was
chosen, not for himself, but for his wealth or his
title. Now, if *I* suspected that, it would make
my house a jail, every hour of my life ghastly, my
very self odious to me. It would make me utterly
wicked; bad enough to be jealous of a human
rival, though death may remove that. But to be
jealous of your own circumstances, to know that
you were nothing in the heart of your beloved,
and they everything; that they had duped you;
that your wooing was an imposture, and your
partner a phantom. That anything like that
should be my lot, Heaven forbid! It never shall.
But were I a man, and found it so, I should load
a pistol, and lie, soon enough, in my last strait
bed."

"Only think how cruel and impossible this is,"
he said, gently, looking into her face. "I ask
you to be reasonable, and consider the consequences
of your pitiless theory. As to wealth, isn't there
always some inequality—and do you mean that an

artificial social distinction should throw asunder for ever two people——"

"I mean to say this—I ought to beg your pardon for interrupting you, but I speak for myself—if I were a man, I could never trust the love of the woman who, being immensely poorer than I, and in an inferior place in life, consented to marry me. I never could; and the more I loved her the worse it would be."

" We are all lawgivers and law-breakers," says he.

"I'm not, for one; I observe, at least, my own precepts; and so resolved, I shall never either love or marry."

He looked at her sadly; he looked down. Even this was more tolerable than if she had said she could neither love nor marry *him*.

" I wish, God knows, that *I* could rule my heart so," he said, sadly.

" Every one who pleases can. There are good nuns and good monks. It is a matter of will and of situation. Man or girl, it is all the same; if they know they can't marry, and have a particle of reason, they see that liking and loving, except in the way of common goodwill, is not for them. They resist that demon Asmodeus, or Cupid, or call him how you please, and he troubles them no more."

" How can you talk so cruelly ?" he says.

There is pain in every line of his handsome face, in the vexed light of the eyes that gaze so piercingly on her, in the uneasy grasp of his hand that leans upon the rough bark of the great tree which her shoulder touches lightly.

CHAPTER X.

FAREWELL.

As men who, in stories, have fallen in love with phantoms, Marston feels, alas! he is now in love with a beautiful image of apathy. Is the great gulf really between them, and he yearning for the impossible?

"If by any sacrifice I could ever make myself the least worthy of you; if you could ever like me ever so little——"

She laughed, but not unkindly.

"If I liked you, or were at all near liking you, you should know it by a certain sign," she says, with a smile, though a sad one.

"How? Do tell me how—how I should know

it?"   And he works off a great piece of the old
bark with his sinewy hand as he talks.

"By my instantly leaving you," she answered.
"And now we have talked sufficiently, haven't we,
on this interesting theme?   One day or other
you'll say, if, by chance, you remember this talk
under the walls of Wybourne, 'That wise but
threadbare young lady was right, and I was
wrong, and it is very well there was some prudent
person near to save me from an irreparable folly;'
and having made this prediction, and said my say
on what seems to me a very simple question, the
subject is, for me, exhausted, and becomes a bore,
and nothing shall tempt me to say or listen to
another word upon it.   What a sudden curious fog
there was yesterday evening?"

Mr. Marston talked of the fog, as well as he
was able, and of the old city of Chester, and whatever else this young lady pleased; he was hardly
half thinking of these themes.   His mind was
employed, in an undercurrent, upon far more
interesting matter.

"Suffering," he thinks, "is the parent of all that
is fine in character.   This girl thinks, resolves,
and acts for herself.   How different she is from
the youthful daughters of luxury!   What origin-
ality—what energy—what self-reliance!"

Perhaps he is right.   This young lady has a

will of her own; she is a little eccentric; she thinks, without much knowledge of the world, very resolutely for herself. I don't know that she is more jealous than other women. But she is an imperious little princess.

While she is trifling in this cruel way, Miss Max comes through a little gate in the hedge at the foot of this sloping field. Urged apparently by the shortness of the time that remained, the young gentleman made one other venture.

"And do you mean to say, Miss Maud, that you, for instance, could never love a man whose rank you thought above your own?"

This was a rather abrupt transition from Carl Maria von Weber, about whose music the young lady was talking.

"You don't keep treaties, it seems," said the young lady; "but as only two or three minutes remain, and we may never meet again, I'll answer you. Yes, perhaps I could. All the more readily for his superiority, all the more deeply for his sacrifices. But in some of my moods, vain or ambitious, I might marry him without caring a pin about him. There are the two cases, and I am never likely to be tempted by either, and—pray, let me say the rest—if I were, no one should ever suspect it, and I should, assuredly, accept neither."

" You said we were never likely to meet again," said the young man. " Is that kind? What have I done to deserve so much severity?"

He glanced down the slope. Miss Max was toiling up. She was stumbling over the twisted roots that spread under the great trees, and seeing a man conversing with her young cousin, she had put up her parasol to keep the slanting sunlight from her eyes, and aid her curious scrutiny.

She could not reach them well in less than four minutes more.

Four minutes still. Precious interval.

" You go to the ball at Wymering?" she asked in a tone that had something odd in it; a strange little sigh, and yet how much apathy.

" Anywhere—yes, certainly," he replies, in hot haste. " Is there a chance—the least hope?"

He remembered that she was not a very likely person to figure at a ball, and so he ended, " I have often intended going there; any hope of your being in the neighbourhood of Wymering about that time?"

" You see, I don't pretend to be a great person. No fairy has bedizened me for an occasion. I have no magnificence to dissolve at a fated hour," she said, with a sad little laugh. " Those balls are not such ill-natured things after all. They help poor girls who work at their needles. Yes, I always go to that, at least as far as the cloak-room."

"Wherever you go, Miss Maud, there will be no one like you; no one like you, anywhere, in all the world; and remember—though you can't like me now—how I adore you."

"Stop—don't talk so to me," she replied. "You are rich. I am, what I am; and language that might be only audacious if we were equals, is insult now."

"Good Heavens! won't you understand me? I only meant, I can't help saying it, that I care to win no one else on earth, and never shall. If you but knew——"

"What need I know more than I do? I believe, rather from your looks than from your words, that you talk your folly in good faith. But I have heard too much of that, for one day. One thing more I have to say, you must leave this immediately; and, if from Miss Max, or any other person, you try to make out anything more, ever so little, about me, about my story, name, business, than I have told you, you never speak to me one word more. That's understood. Here now is my cousin."

Miss Max, smiling pleasantly, said:

"Dear me, Mr. Marston, who could have fancied that you would have been here! I could not think who it could be, as I came up the hill. Were you at Wybourne Church?"

"Oh, no! I wai——" He was going to say, "waited outside," but he corrected himself. "I arrived too late. A pretty little church it seems to be."

"Oh! quite a beautiful little church, inside. Some one showed you the path here, I suppose; those up there are the ruins of old Wybourne Hall: what an awful fog we had last night! Do you know, it was really quite frightful going through it at the fearful speed we did. You must come and drink tea with us, Mr. Marston."

"No, dear, we must not have any one to tea to-night; I have particular reasons, and besides, Mr. Marston has to leave this immediately," said Miss Maud, inhospitably.

He looked at her ruefully.

"You told me you were going immediately?" said the young lady, gently, but with a slight emphasis.

"But I dare say you can manage to put it off for an hour or so, Mr. Marston—can't you?" asked Miss Max.

He glanced at the inexorable Miss Maud, and he read his doom in that pretty face.

"I'm afraid—it is so very kind of you—but

I'm really afraid it is quite impossible," he answers.·

" I don't like to bore you, Mr. Marston ; but if you *can* stay to tea, just an hour or two—can't you manage that ? I shall be *so* glad," urged the old lady.

" Mr. Marston, I believe, made a promise to be at another place this evening," said the girl ; "and Mr. Marston says he prides himself on keeping his word."

Though she was looking down at the grass, and said this with something like a smile, and in a careless way, Mr. Marston dares not disobey the reminder it conveys.

"That is perfectly true, what Miss Maud says. I made that promise to a person whom I dare not disappoint, whom I respect more than I can describe," and he added in a low tone to Maud, " whom it is my pride to obey."

" Good-bye, Mr. Marston," she says with a smile, extending her pretty hand very frankly.

How he felt as he touched it !

" Good-bye, Miss Max," he says, turning with a sigh and a smile to that lady.

" Good-bye, since so it must be, and I hope we may chance to meet again, Mr. Marston," said the old lady, kindly giving him her thin old hand.

"So do I—so do I—thank you, very much,"
says he, and he pauses, looking as if he was not
sure that he had not something more to say.

"Good-bye, Miss Max," he repeats, "and good-
bye," he says again to the girl, extending his
hand.

Once more, for a second or two, he holds her
hand in his, and then he finds himself walking
quickly under the straggling hawthorns. The
sprays are rattling on his hat as he crosses the
stile. He is striding through the first narrow
field over which his walk from the church had
been. Lifeless and dimmed the hedges are, and
the songs of the birds all round are but a noise
which he scarcely hears. There is but one thought
in his brain and heart, as he strides through this
cloistered solitude, as swiftly as if his rate of travel
could shorten the time between this and the ball
at Wymering.

This Mr. Marston was not so much a fool as
not to know that, being a man of honour, he had
taken a very serious step. The young lady—for
be her troubles and distresses what they might, a
lady she surely was—whom he had pursued so far,
and to whom he had spoken in language quite
irrevocable, had now, in her small hand, his fate
and fortunes.

There seemed to walk beside him, along his

grassy path, an angry father, and the sneers and gabble of kindred, who had a right to talk, were barking and laughing at his heels. He knew very well what he had to count upon, and had known it all along. But it did not daunt him, either then or now.

Here was his first love, and an idol not created by his fancy, but, undoubtedly, the most beautiful girl he had ever seen. A first love devouring material so combustible; a generous fellow, impetuous, sanguine, dominated by imagination, and who had delivered eloquent lectures upon the folly of political economy, and the intrinsic tyranny of our social system.

These things troubled him, no doubt; but thus beset, he had no more notion of turning about than had honest Christian and Hopeful as they plodded through the Valley of the Shadow of Death. He felt, I dare say, pretty much as a knight when riding into the lists to mortal combat for the mistress of his heart.

He held himself now, so far as his own personal case went, irrevocably betrothed to his beautiful but cruel mistress; and so far from halting between two opinions, if what had passed this evening had been still unsaid, he would have gone round the world for a chance of speaking it.

Literally abiding by his promise, he left Wybourne as suddenly as he came.

Miss Max looked after him as the underwood hid him from view, with the somewhat blank and ruminating countenance which belongs to the lady about whose ears a favourite castle in the air has just tumbled.

"Well," said she, turning to her young companion, nodding, and looking wise, "that gentleman is gone on a fool's errand, I venture to say. Have you any idea where he's gone?"

"Not the least."

"I liked him very much. I hope he's not going to make a fool of himself. I really thought he liked you. He is so full of romance. See how you blush!"

"I always do when I think I shall, and when I particularly wish not," she said, with a smile, but a little vexed.

"Well, I suspect, from what he said, that he is going to ask some young lady an interesting question; or, perhaps, he is actually engaged; goodness knows."

Miss Max was walking under the lordly trees towards home and tea, with her young cousin beside her.

"That's a blackbird," she says, listening for a moment. "What a delicious evening!"

"Has your mother set out again upon her usual mysterious journey?" inquired Miss Max.

"I fancy not—not yet, at least," answered the girl, listlessly.

"Well, I may say to you, I can't understand your mother the least, my dear."

The girl made no answer: she was looking up, with a listless and sad face, toward the fleecy clouds that now glowed in the tint of sunset, and the rooks, that make no holiday of Sunday, winging homeward, high in air, with a softened cawing.

CHAPTER XI.

ROYDON.

NEXT day, about noon, the young lady, with an embrace, and a little shower of kisses, took a loving farewell of her cousin, stepped into a fly, with her boxes on the roof, and, with a sad heart, began her journey homeward.

It was a good way, some thirty miles and upwards. She had borrowed Miss Max's novel, grew tired of it a dozen times, and resumed it as often, and as she neared home, with the restlessness that accompanies the conclusion of a journey, she threw her book on the opposite cushion, and looked out of the window, greeting, as it were, the familiar objects that in succession presented themselves to view.

Now they are passing the windmill on the little hillock overlooking the road. The day is sultry. There is not a breath to stir its sails, and the great arms stand bare and motionless. Mill and hillock glide backward, and are gone.

The road descends a little. They are between files of old elms. It grows broader; there stands the old village tree, with a rude wooden bench encircling its trunk. The time-honoured tree sails back, and is lost, and quaint old diamond-latticed houses float into view, and pass. Here and there a familiar face is seen at door or window, or peeping from the shade over the hatch; and the girl, from the fly-window, nods and smiles. They are now midway in the quiet little street, but they have not yet reached the home that she loves not.

At the other side are the stained walls of an antique church; the gilded vane, the grey tomb-stones, spread over the thick emerald grass, and the yew-tree, all go slanting off, hurry-scurry, as the fly-wheels whirl, by a wide circuit, through the piers of a great iron gate, which has just given egress to an old-fashioned family coach.

It is going the other way. It does not pass her. It and its liveried footmen are fast getting into perspective under the boughs of the trees that line the road. Through the window of the fly, as it turns, she has a momentary peep.

"Brown and gold," she says, as listlessly she leans back again in her humble conveyance. "The Tinterns. And so here I am, a black sheep, a scamp, and a reprobate, come home again, as curses do!"

There was not much remorse, but a good deal of bitterness in her tone, and the girl yawned, with her finger-tips to her lips, and looked for a moment a little peevish.

There is what is termed technically an "approach" to the house up to which she is driving, a serpentine road, two miles long at least, through a wooded demesne. But, wisely, the old owner of Roydon, when consulting his new lights, and laying out, according to picturesque principles, the modern approach, would not allow them to obliterate or alter the old avenue of the mansion— broad and straight, something more than a quarter of a mile long, with a double line of trees at each side, wide enough apart to admit the entire front of the building.

It is up this broad, straight avenue she is driving now.

A lazy man, with a mind at ease, entering here for the first time, looking up the solemn lines of

enormous boughs to the old-world glories that
close the perspective, escaping from the vulgar
world of dust and rattle into shorn grass and
clear, silent air, and the luxurious and melancholy
grandeur of all that surrounds him, might fancy
himself in the "delicious land" once visited by
the enchanted Sir Jeofry.

In the distance rises a grand Elizabethan struc-
ture—broad, florid, built of white stone, yellowed
and many-tinted by time. A vague effect fills
the eye of pinnacles and bell-mouthed chimneys,
and curved and corniced gables, balustrades, a
front variously indented and projecting: multi-
tudes of stone-shafted windows, deep-curved scrolls,
and heraldic shields and supporters; a broad flight
of steps, and then another balustrade running at
both sides the whole length of the base. All this
rises before her, with its peculiar combination of
richness, lightness, and solidity, basking drowsily
in the summer sun.

As you approach, you discern a wide court-
yard in front, with a second line of balustrade
nearer to you.

On the summit of this, here and there, are
peacocks sunning themselves, some white, others
plumed in their proper gold and purple. They nod
their crested heads as they prune their plumage.

and hang their long tails to the grass, disturbing
the slumbrous air, now and then, with a discordant
scream.

As you draw nearer still, before you enter the
court, two oblong ponds reveal their spacious
waters, at the right and the left; you may hear
the shower of the fountains playing in the middle,
snowy coronals of water-lilies are floating near
their banks, and swans are grandly gliding round
and up and down.

Now the homely "fly" is in the court-yard. A
great Russian dog lies sunning himself on the
dazzling gravel, near the steps, and whacks the
ground twice or thrice with his tail, in lazy recognition, as he sees the young lady look from the
window of her homely vehicle.

"I suppose that is the way of the world, Bevis,"
she says; "you know whom to get up for."

Her attention is arrested by a carriage waiting
a little way from the steps.

"That's the dean," comments the young lady as
she sees that very neat equipage, at the window of
which a tall footman, in light blue and gold livery,
with powdered hair, is standing. He has just
descended the broad flight of steps under the
great shield which overhangs the door, and which
displays in high relief all the heraldic insignia of
that branch of the Vernons. He is delivering a

message from Lady Vernon—Barbara Vernon—I give you the christian name of this famous widow at once, as it is mentioned often in the sequel—to an old lady sitting in the carriage.

Old Miss Wyvel, the dean's sister, as usual, with her feet on a pan of hot water, sits in the carriage reading her novel, and nursing her rheumatism, while her brother, the dean, makes his visit, with an apology from her for not coming in.

"We'll not mind Miss Wyvel this time. She'll be all the happier that I don't disturb her, and so shall I."

Another tall footman, seeing who is in the fly, descends the broad steps quickly, and opens the door.

"The Dean of Chartry is here?" inquires the young lady. "How long has he been here?"

"About ten minutes, please, miss."

"Any other visitor?"

"No one, miss, at present, please."

"Where is her ladyship?"

"In the library, please, miss."

"Will you tell somebody, please, to tell my maid that I want her in my room?" said the young lady.

And she ran up the steps lightly, and entered the great hall. It runs back into space, almost into darkness, with oak panelled walls and tall pictures. She turned to the right, where the broad oak staircase ascends.

Up she runs. There are more portraits in this house, one must suppose, than the owners well know what to do with, for you can hardly turn a corner without meeting a gentleman with rosettes in his shoes, a ruff round his neck, and a rapier by his side, or a lady in the toilet of Queen Elizabeth. All ages, indeed, of English costume, from the court of Harry the Eighth down to George the Second, are represented here; and, I suspect, there is now not a soul on earth who could tell you the names of all these magnificos and high dames, who are fain to lurk behind corners, or stand in their frames, with their backs against the walls of galleries, passed, back and forward, by gabbling moderns, who don't care twopence about them or their finery.

Off one of these galleries the young lady enters her own room—stately, comfortable, luxurious— looks around with a good-natured recognition, and has hardly begun to take off her dusty things, and prepare to make her toilet, when her maid passes in through the dressing-room door, smiling.

CHAPTER XII.

BARBARA VERNON.

By no means old is this maid. Some six-and-thirty years, perhaps. She has carried Maud in her arms when she was a little thing, and dressed her; sat by her bed and told her fairy-tales in the nursery.

"Welcome home, Miss Maud," smiles Jones.

"And how have you been?" says the young lady, taking her by the hand, and kissing her affectionately on one cheek and the other. "As for me, I've been flourishing. I almost think, old Jones, if I had only had you with me, I should never have come back again."

"La, miss, how you talk!"

"I've been leading a wild, free life. Did you

ever see so much dust, Jones, on any human being?"

"Indeed, you are in a pickle, miss. Charles said you came in a fly with one horse. I wonder her ladyship did not send a carriage to Wybourne to meet you."

"Mamma has other things and people to think about," said the young lady, a little bitterly. "But I dare say if I had asked I should have had it; though, indeed, I shouldn't have liked it."

"Your hand's all sunburnt, miss."

"I've been sketching; and I never could sketch with a glove on."

"Well, dear me, it *was* a fancy going in these queer things! Why, I would not be seen in such things myself, miss, much less you. You'd best bundle off that dress, miss, as quick as you can. La! it is thick with dust. Phiew!"

"Help me, Jones, help me." And as she continued her toilet she asked: "Is mamma yet talking of making her usual journey?"

"Not a word, miss, of any one stirring yet. Norris would know. She has not heard nothing."

"The Tinterns' carriage was here to-day—I passed it at the gate. Do you know who called?"

"Mr. Tintern and Mrs. They was here nigh half an hour. Leave them alone for 'aving their eyes about 'em, miss. There ain't a tack druv in

the house, or a slate loose, but its known down at
the Grange before it's noticed here."

" I think, Jones, they reckon upon—don't pull
my hair." By this time she was sitting in her
dressing-gown before the glass, with her dark,
golden-brown hair hanging over her shoulders in
such profusion, that it seemed incredible how such
masses could find growing room in one little head.
Jones was brushing out its folds.

" I'm not pulling it, indeed, miss," she protested.

" Yes, you were, Jones. Don't ever contradict
me. Has either of my special horrors—Mr. Smelt
—he's the clergyman or dissenter, something in
black, the sleek fat man that comes so often—has
he been here since ? "

" He may 'ave, miss; but——"

· " But you don't know. Well, the other —
Doctor Malkin ? "

" Oh, dear yes, miss. He was here, please, on
Friday last."

·· You're sure ? "

" Yes, miss, please. Her ladyship sent for me
to the shield room. She only asked whether I
could remember for certain, miss, what day you
were to return 'ome to Wybourne with Miss
Medwyn."

" Well ? "

" Well, miss, she had it down in a book, and

read it to me, and I said 'twas right. You said early—the seventeenth."

"And did she say anything more?"

"No, please, miss, nothing more. Only she said, 'That's all, you need not wait.'"

"And what about Doctor Malkin?"

"He was showed in, miss, please, just as I was going out. And I heard her order Edward not to let any visitor in; and that was all, please."

"Do you know the name of this place, parish, and county, Jones?" says the young lady, carelessly.

"Well, I ought to by this time, miss," laughs Jones.

"I don't think you do. The name of this place is Bœotia, and it is famous for its dulness, and Doctor Malkin is one of the six inhabitants who can think and talk a little. He is an agreeable man, and—put a pin there—an unpleasant-looking man. I like talking to him; but I think, on the whole, I should not be sorry if he were laid in the Red Sea, as poor nurse Creswell used to say. What do you think of him?"

"That is a gentleman, Heaven forgive me, I can't abide, miss," answered Jones. "I hate his face. I always feel in low spirits after I see it."

"Well, anything more?" continues Miss Maud.

"When are the people coming to hear grandpapa's will read?"

"To-morrow, I believe, miss. But, as yet, Mr. Eccles has not got no orders about it. He said so after dinner in the 'ouse-keeper's room yesterday."

"And is there anything going to be—a tea and plum-cake for the school-children, or a meeting of missionaries, or anything of any kind?"

"Nothing, miss, please, as I 'ave heard of, but——"

"You'll knock down that china, Jones."

"What, miss?"

"My ring-stand—my Dresden dancers."

"Oh! The little man and woman with one arm akimbo and the other up. I saw them all the time."

"Well, take great care. I'm sure I shall kill you if you break them. You were going to tell me there is nothing going to be, except something —what is it?"

"Oh! I know; yes, miss, the conseckeration of the monument in the church. That will be to-morrow evening, miss."

"Oh! Really? Well, that *was* a whim! Give me those ear-rings. No, *not* those—the others; not those either. Don't you see the little ones. Thanks. Yes. I must run down and see mamma,

I suppose, though I'm very sure she doesn't care if she did not see my face for a year, or—for ever."

"La, miss! you must not talk like that. Your mamma's a very religious lady—the most so, as every one knows, in the county—I might say in all England—and it's just her way; the same with every one, a little bit high and distant like; but it ain't fit, miss, you should say that."

"No, Jones, we can't agree, mamma and I. Give me that small enamel brooch—the little one with the lady's head set in gold. Thanks. She does not like me"—the young lady was standing before the glass, and I dare say was well pleased, for she looked splendidly handsome —" and the reason is just this, every one else flatters her. You and all the other sneaks. I never do, although I am sometimes a little afraid of her like the rest. I'm nervous, I don't know why; but it's not cowardice. I never flatter her."

"No, miss, it ain't that; it's only you don't try her. You won't go the right way about it."

"There's no use, Jones—you only vex me. I've often felt that I would give the world to throw my arms about her neck and kiss her; but some-how I can't; she won't let me. Perhaps she tries; but she can't love me; and so it always was, as far back as I can remember, and so it will always be, and I've made up my mind to it; it can't be helped."

So Miss Maud Vernon walked along the gallery, and went down the broad stairs, passing many ancestors who stood by, at the right and the left, against the wall, as she did so, and singing low to herself as she went, with a clear and rich voice, an Italian air quite new to the solemn people in the picture-frames, at whom she looked listlessly, thinking neither of them nor of her song as she passed by.

Mr. Tarpey, the groom of the chambers, was fussing with the decorations of the hall as she passed.

"Can you tell me where her ladyship is?" she inquired.

"Her ladyship, I think, is still in the library. Please, shall I see, miss?"

"Don't mind. I'll try myself. Is her ladyship alone?"

"I think so, miss."

He crossed the hall, and opened the second door from the great entrance, which stood wide open, in this sultry weather, by Lady Vernon's command, the two tall footmen, in their blue and gold liveries, keeping guard there.

Maud glanced through the open hall-door as she crossed the hall; she would have been rather pleased to see a carriage approaching; she did not care for a very long interview with her mother; but there was no sign of a visitor in sight.

"Thanks, I'll go alone," she said, dispensing with the escort of Mr. Tarpey; and passing through two spacious rooms, she reached the door of the library. Lady Vernon treated that apartment as her private cabinet, and from her childhood Maud had been accustomed to respect it.

Maud has no liking for the coming interview. She would, now, have liked to put it off, and as she crosses the Turkey carpet that muffles her tread, her step slackens. She stops at the door and raises her hand to knock, but she doesn't knock; she hesitates; she has a great mind to turn back, and wait till her mother sends for her. But, perhaps, that would not do. She has been at home nearly an hour, and it is time she should ask Lady Vernon how she does.

She knocks at the door, and hears a clear voice call "Come in."

She turns the handle accordingly, and steps into a spacious room, hung with gilded leather; the blinds are down, the sun by this time shining on this side of the house, and a mellow, cathedral-like dimness prevails. There are three or four antique bookcases, carved in ponderous relief, through the leaves and scrolls of which are grinning grotesque and ugly faces, rich with a cynical Gothic fancy, and overhung by fantastic cornices, crowned with the heraldic shield and supporters of the Vernons. They are stored with gilded volumes; portraits hang here, as in other parts of this rich old house, and cold marble busts gleam on pedestals from the corners.

Sitting at a table in the middle of this room is a very handsome woman of forty years or upwards, with skin smooth as ivory, and jet-black hair, divided in the middle, and brought down over her white temples and small pretty ears smoothly in the simple classic fashion, now out of date. Her finely pencilled black eyebrows, and her features with a classic elegance of outline, carry an expression of cold hauteur. Her slight embonpoint becomes her grave but rich dress, which is that of a woman of rank and wealth, by no means indifferent to the impression produced by externals.

This lady, with one handsome foot upon a stool, and a desk before her, is in a leisurely way writing a letter, over which she bends just the least thing in the world. Her pose is decidedly elegant.

The lady glances slightly toward the door. Her large grey eyes, under their long lashes, rest for a moment on her daughter. She does not smile; the pen is still in her fingers. She says, simply, in her clear and rather sweet tones, " Oh, Maud ?   I will speak to you in a few minutes, when I have

put this into its envelope. Won't you sit down?"
And so she continues to write.

The young lady flashes back a rather fiery
glance in return for this cool welcome, and does
not sit down, but walks instead, with a quick step,
to the window, pulls the blind aside, and looks out
perseveringly.

CHAPTER XIII.

MOTHER AND DAUGHTER.

LADY VERNON having enclosed and addressed her letter, added it to the little pack of about six others at her left. Then looking up, she said :

"So, you are quite well, Maud, and you arrived at a quarter past three?"

"Quite well, mamma, thanks. I suppose it was about that time; and I hope you are very well."

"I am well, thanks; and I wished to mention that when you, as you told me, fixed the seventeenth for your return to the Hermitage with Maximilla Medwyn, I was under a mistake, and did not see, till too late, that the seventeenth would be Sunday; and I should not have given my sanction to your travelling for pleasure on Sunday. I wished to mention that particularly. I told Maximilla I should be happy to receive her any day this week. Is she coming, do you know?"

"She would have come with me this morning, but she had so much to say to her servants, and so many things to arrange, that she could not leave home till after dinner at soonest, so she hopes to be here at ten to-night; and if anything should happen to prevent her, you are to have a note, by post, in the morning."

"She will be in time, at all events, for the bishop's sermon to-morrow," says Lady Vernon. "The monument will be uncovered at five o'clock. The bishop arrives at six. He has to consecrate the new church at Eastover, before he comes here, and then he goes on, after his sermon, to Ward-lake, for the evening meeting of the church missions."

Miss Vernon is hardly so much interested in all this as her mother is, although even she recites the programme a little dryly. But dry as is her recital, it is not often that she volunteers so much information to her daughter.

"And what can the bishop have to say about the monument, to lead him so much out of his way, poor old man?"

"The bishop seems to think that his having been the dearest friend that Mr. Howard had on earth, constitutes some little claim upon him," says Lady Vernon, haughtily, in a cold tone, and with her fine grey eyes fixed on her daughter.

"Oh! I did not know," says Maud, a little apologetically.

"No, of course you did not; you seldom do know, or care to know, anything that interests me," says the elder lady, with her fine brows a little higher. ·

Maud coloured suddenly, with an impatient movement of her head. She was not sitting down, only standing near the table, drumming on it with her finger-tops, and she felt for a moment as if she could have stamped.

She answered, however, without any show of excitement except in her brilliant colour and eyes.

"I did not know, mamma, that this monument to Mr. Howard interested you particularly."

"No, not particularly," said handsome Lady Vernon, sternly, for she was one of those persons who don't brook contradiction, and who interpret discussion as a contradiction. "Mr. Howard was the best vicar we ever had here, or ever shall have; and, in his way, a benefactor to this parish. The bishop, who admired and loved him, as much as one man could another, suggested that for such a man, in the field of his labours, having lain in his grave more than a score of years unrecorded by a single line, it was time that a monument should be raised. He wished a beautiful one, and so I believe it is. His name is first in the list of subscribers, and it is his idea, and it is he who has taken a lead in it; and, therefore, though interested, I am not particularly interested in the personal degree which your emphasis would imply."

"Well, all I can say is, I'm very unlucky, mamma."

"I think you are unlucky," replied her mother, coldly, turning her head slowly away, and looking at the pendule over the chimney.

"Have you anything to ask me, Maud?" inquired Lady Vernon, after a little interval.

"Nothing, thanks, mamma," said Maud, with her head a little high. "I'm afraid I have bored you coming in when you were busy. But having been away ten days, I thought it would have been wrong, or at least odd, if I had not come to see you to ask you how you were."

"So it would," said Lady Vernon. "Will you touch the bell?"

She did so.

"Well, mamma, I suppose there's nothing more?"

"Nothing, Maud."

Maud's heart swelled with bitterness as she left the room, and shut the door gently.

"No father, no mother, no near relation!" she thought, impetuously. "I love cousin Max better than fifty such mammas. There are girls who would hate her. But I can't. Why am I cursed with this cruel yearning for her love? And she can't love me—she won't have my love. I think she wishes me to hate her."

When Maud was a little thing, as far back as she could remember, her idea of a "mamma" was an embodiment of power, and something to be afraid of. Seldom seen except when the spirited little girl became unmanageable; then there would be a rustling of silk and a flutter of lace in the nursery, and the handsome figure, the proud still face and large grey eyes were before her. This phantom instantly awed her. It always looked severe, and never smiled, and its sweet cold tones were dreadful. The child's instinct could see dislike, hidden from maturer observers, in those fine eyes, and never heard a tender note in that harmonious voice.

Miss Maud passed out through the suite of rooms, and encountered Lady Vernon's footman going in to take her letters.

In the hall, serious Mr. Eccles, the gentleman-like butler, was passing upon his business with the quiet importance and gravity of office.

The young lady had a word to say.

"Is any one expected to dinner to-day?"

"Yês, miss—five; the vicar and Mrs. Foljambe; his curate, the Reverend Mr. Doody; and Mr. Puntles and Doctor Malkin. There was an invitation for Captain Bamme; but he is absent on militia business, and it is thought not probable, miss, he will return in time."

Anything was better than a tête-à-tête with Lady Vernon; a situation which Lady Vernon herself seemed to deprecate as strongly as her daughter, for it did not occur usually six times in a year.

CHAPTER XIV.

GUESTS AND NEIGHBOURS.

WHEN, that evening, Miss Maud entered the vast drawing-room, it was some minutes past eight. The outer world was in twilight, but lamps glowed faintly here, upon the thick silken curtains, and lofty mirrors, and pictures, and treasures of china, and upon figures of people assembled for dinner. The little party was almost lost in the great void, as Miss Maud made her journey, over a comparatively gloomy desert of thick carpet, to the group illuminated by the soft light of the lamps.

Tall old Mr. Foljambe, the vicar, was entertaining Lady Vernon with his bland and dignified conversation. Doctor Malkin would have liked that post, but the vicar came first, and seized it.

The vicar is a well-connected old gentleman, related, in some remote cousinship, to the late Sir Amyrald Vernon, and knows very well what he is about. Has not Lady Vernon, the relict of that lamented kinsman, two extremely desirable livings in her gift, besides smaller things? And, old as the Reverend Mr. Foljambe is, are not the incumbents of these fat fields of usefulness older still? Is not the Reverend Mr. Cripry seventy-nine? And is not the venerable Doctor Shanks eighty-two, by the records of Trinity College, Cambridge? Compared with these mature ornaments of the Church, the vicar justly feels himself a stripling; and being a young fellow, not yet in his seventy-first year, he may well complain of a selfish longevity which is sacrificing the interests of two important parishes which require a vigorous ministration.

The vicar's shrewd old eye, from its wrinkled corners, observes Doctor Malkin's wistful look, and knows from experience that he likes to take possession of Lady Vernon's ear, and has suffered more than once from the tenacity with which he keeps it, when he can, to himself.

"Nothing of the kind shall happen to-night," thinks the vicar, who, having a handsome bit of money in consols, has sold out a hundred pounds

to invest in a subscription to the monument of his
predecessor, the Reverend Mr. Howard—a good
work in which Lady Vernon takes a warm
interest, as she always does in anything she
takes up.

The vicar has her fast upon this, and the doctor
thinks he can read sly triumph in his eye, as, once
or twice, it glides over to him, and their glances
meet for a moment.

" Well, doctor, and how's all wid you?" inquires
the Reverend Michael Doody, with a grin that
shows his fine white fangs, and a trifling clap of
his enormous hand on the doctor's shoulder.
" Elegant, I suppose?"

The doctor's slight frame quivers under the
caress of the cleric, but he smiles politely; for
who knows what influence this new importation
may grow to in this part of the world?

" I'm very well, thanks—as well as a fellow, so
much knocked about as a doctor, can be in this
hot weather."

The doctor is a little bald, with a high pale
nose, a long upper lip, a receding chin, very
blue, and a pair of fine dark eyes, set too close
together, and with a slight obliquity which spoils
them a great deal, and does not improve his
countenance; his shirt-front is beautified with
needlework, and his rather tall choker, for his neck

is long, is made up by his exemplary laundress
with a snowy smoothness worthy of the neatness
and decision with which the doctor ties it.

"My governor, the vicar, has Lady Vernon fast
by the button," continued Mr. Doody, with something like a wink. "She must be a very conscientious woman, to listen so well to her clergy.
He was talking about Vicar Howard's monument
when I was near them, just now."

The doctor laughed and shrugged, and Mr.
Doody thought for a moment he squinted a little
more than usual.

"Our good vicar has but one subject at
present," says the doctor, who gives Mr. Doody,
as a stranger, credit for a good deal of waggish
penetration. "You have heard of the clarionet-
man who had but one tune, and played it always
through the key-hole, till it answered its purpose,
and extracted a gratuity; and he made it pay very
well, I believe."

"And rayther hard, doctor, that you can't get
your turn at the key-hole, eh, my boy?"

And the reverend gentleman utters a stentorian
giggle, and pokes his finger on the doctor's ribs.

"I don't quite see, Mr. Doody," says Doctor
Malkin, with a very creditable smile, all things
considered.

"Boo, docthor, my darlin' fellow, don't be

comin' the simpleton over us. Don't we both know that every man in your profession likes to stand well with the women? And here you are, and if it was to make a man of ye, not a word can ye edge in. It's too hard, docthor, that the man of death should be blocked out by a tombstone. Be the powers, it ain't fair! He's takin' her all over the monument; up on the pedestal, over the cornice, down in the vault! It's an unfair advantage. But, never mind, my boy, ye'll be even with him yet; ye'll attind him in his next indisposition."

This pleasant banter was accompanied by a running explosion of giggles; and while the tall and rather handsome Irishman is enjoying his little bit of farce, with intense relish, the vicar and Lady Vernon are discoursing thus:

"I thought, Lady Vernon, you would like, of course, in the most private way in the world, to collect opinion upon the monument; so, as he draws very nicely, my wife says, I allowed my curate, Mr. Doody, just in the strictest privacy, quite to ourselves, you understand, a peep at it, for about five minutes, this morning. He thinks it very fine indeed—very fine—as, indeed, every one who has seen it does. There is, I fancy, but one opinion. I wish so much, Lady Vernon, I might venture to invite you to pay my church—

yours, indeed, I might more properly call it—a visit to-morrow, to look at what I may term your beautiful gift to the sacred edifice."

"No, thanks; I shall see it time enough."

"But, as it owes its existence, Lady Vernon, to your extremely munificent subscription——"

"I thought it was due, as the bishop said, to a very good clergyman," says Lady Vernon, quietly cutting it short; "and I gave what I thought right. That is all. And so your curate draws?"

"I'm nothing of a draughtsman myself, but my wife understands it, and says he draws extremely nicely."

"That tall young man, is he?"

"I ought to have presented him, Lady Vernon. It was an omission—an inexcusable omission—a very inexcusable omission." He was trying to catch his curate's eye all this time. "He has been with me only a week, and yesterday he did duty at Loxton. You remember, Lady Vernon, you thought an Irishman would answer best."

"The bishop says he has found them extremely energetic, and for very hard work unrivalled."

"He's a very rough diamond, I must admit. But he's a convert from Romanism, and a very laborious young man, and a good scholar."

He had beckoned Mr. Doody to approach, and accordingly that herculean labourer in the apostolic field drew near, a head and shoulders above all the other guests. The tall old vicar alone was sitting.

"Allow me, Lady Vernon, to present my curate, Mr. Doody," says the vicar, rising to do the honours.

Mr. Doody is not the least overcome by the honour. His fine eyes have examined the lady, of whom he had heard so much, but of whom he has not had so near a view before, with the grave curiosity with which he would have scrutinised an interesting piece of waxwork.

The florid young man, with black whiskers and glossy black head, makes his best bow gravely, and inquires unexpectedly:

"How are ye, ma'am? A good evening, Lady Vernon." A form of salutation with which it is his wont, as it were, to clench an introduction.

Lady Vernon does not mind answering or reciprocating these rather oddly placed greetings, but talks a few sentences with him, and then turns again to the vicar, and the curate, after a little wait, turns on his heel, and seeks employment for his active mind elsewhere.

Let me not be imagined to present an average Irish curate. Mr. Doody is almost as great a prodigy at home as anywhere else. His father, with his own hands, in his bare shins, with a

dhuddeen stuck in his caubeen, cuts turf in the
bog near the famous battle-field of Aghrim.   He
is not a bit ashamed of his father or his belongings.
He holds him to be as good a gentleman as himself—being the lineal descendant of the O'Doody
of Tyr Doody—and himself as good as the primate.
He sends his mother a present every now and
then, but the farm is well stocked, and his parents
are, according to primitive ideas, wealthy people in
their homely way.   His lapse into Protestantism
was, of course, a sore blow.   And when Doctor
Pollard's wife mentioned to the priest, with perhaps a little excusable triumph, that Michael
Doody had embraced the principles of the Refor-
mation, his reverence scratched his tonsure, and
said :

"I'm not a bit surprised, ma'am, for he was
always an impudent chap; but there was some
good in the boy, also; and go where he may at
present, so sure as I'm a Catholic, he'll die one."

CHAPTER XV.

DINNER.

OLD Mr. Foljambe takes precedence, at dinner, in right of his cloth, connexions, and antiquity, and has taken Lady Vernon into the dining-room, and converses assiduously with that great lady.

Maud finds herself between the curate and Doctor Malkin. Middle-aged and agreeable Captain Bamme resents an arrangement which isolates him, and eyes the curate with disgust.

Captain Bamme does not count age by years. He knows better. As long as a fellow looks young, and feels young, he *is* young. The captain smiles more than any other two men in the parish. He is short and square, but he skips and swaggers like an officer and a gentleman. Who can talk to

a girl like Charley Bamme? Who understands
that mixture of gaiety and gallantry—with now
and then a dash of tenderness—like this officer.
To be sure he's not a marrying man; every one
knows that. It is out of the question. The captain laughs with a melancholy scorn over his
scanty pittance. A fourth son, by Jove! and put
to a poor profession. But is he not the life and
soul of a picnic, and the darling of the ladies?

"I've been quartered in Ireland," says little
Captain Bamme, under cover of the surrounding
buzz, to his more fortunate neighbour, Doctor
Malkin; "I've been in every part of it; I have
talked to Irishmen of every rank and occupation,
but such a brogue as that, I give you my honour,
I never heard. Why, they wouldn't have him to
preach to a congregation of carmen in Dublin. I
never heard anything like it. How did old Foljambe light on him? I really think, when people
bring fellows like that to a place like this, where
people *must* know him, and, for anything you or I
can tell, that fellow may spend the rest of his days
down here—by Jove! it's pleasant—they ought to
be prepared to give an account of him. I suppose
Foljambe can say what he is? You never met
such an insufferable creature. I never spoke to
the fellow before in my life; and he came up to

me in the hall here making some vulgar *personal* joke, I give you my honour."

"He seems to succeed very well," says the doctor, "notwithstanding. I suppose there's something interesting in it, though you and I can't perceive it."

"Upon my soul, I can't."

And with this declaration he turns to Mrs. Foljambe, who is at his right, determined to make her account for her intolerable curate.

Mrs. Foljambe is tall, deaf, and melancholy—a woman very nearly useless, and quite harmless.

"I was saying just now to Doctor Malkin," begins the captain, "that I've been, at different times, quartered in Ireland——"

A footman here presents at the captain's right hand an entrée which he loves, and on which he pounces.

"A daughter in Ireland?" repeats the drowsy voice of Mrs. Foljambe, turning her dull and small grey eyes upon him, with a heavy sigh.

"No, ha, ha! not yet; *quartered* in Ireland. No. Time enough for that, I hope. I'm not married, Mrs. Foljambe—thanks, that will do. I say, I have been a little puzzled by your curate's accent." He was speaking low, but with measured articulation; for although the Reverend Michael

Doody's voice is loud and busy at the other side of the table, and the buzz of conversation is general, that odious person's ears, for aught the captain knew, may be preternaturally acute. "And although I know Ireland pretty well — Athlone Limerick, Cork, Dublin, and all that—yet I never heard his accent before in my life."

Mrs. Foljambe bowed her patient grey head, and did not seem aware that any answer was needed.

"Can you say what part of the country he comes from?" persists Captain Bamme.

"I rather think Ireland," replies Mrs. Foljambe, with an effort and another sigh.

"I rather think so myself," says the captain, in a disgusted aside, over his veal and truffles. "The woman knows no more about him than my hat does of snipe-shooting," he says, in the doctor's ear, and drowns his indignation in a glass of hock, which the butler at that moment charitably proffers.

The doctor has now got into talk with Miss Vernon. The captain has no wish to steal good Mrs. Foljambe's bothered ear from old Mr. Puntles, who is labouring to entertain her. So Captain Bamme attends to his dinner with great concentration and energy for some time. It was not until he came to the iced-pudding that he thought of the Reverend Michael Doody again, and his joke upon the captain's stature—"a fellow I had never exchanged six words with before!"— and raising his eyes, he saw, with a qualm, those of the florid divine, fixed jocosely on him from the other side of the table.

"Upon my soul, it is very nearly intolerable!" the captain protests, mentally, as he leans back, with a flushed face. He resolves that this fellow must be snubbed, and laughed at, and sat upon, and taught to know his place, and held at arm's length.

As the captain has, however, nothing clever ready, he prefers not noticing the curate's expression: and throwing into his countenance all the dignity which a not very tragic face can carry, he avails himself of Mr. Eccles's murmur at his right elbow, and takes a glass of sherry.

"I'll drink a glass of wine widgye, captain," insists the curate, recurring to a happily obsolete usage. "Get me some white wine."

The captain bows and stares, with a rather withering condescension and gravity, which, however, does not in the least tell upon the impervious curate, who, his glass replenished, observes with a hilarious smile, "An agreeable way of makin' acquaintance with my flock; better than a dhry domiciliary visit, captain, by a long chalk. I

pledge you, my gallant parishioner—and here's to
our better acquaintance."

The captain nods curtly, and gulps down his
wine, without half tasting it; but even on these
terms he thinks it is well to have escaped that
brute.

Miss Vernon is again talking to the curate.
How disgusting! He turns, without thinking
what he's doing, to his right, and his eyes meet the
dull and innocent gaze of grey Mrs. Foljambe,
who, recalled to the festive scene, makes an effort,
and tells him her only story.

" We knew two very respectable poor women in
this town. Anne Pluggs was one, and her sister,
Julia Pluggs, was the other; there were two.
They had both been servants, cooks, and they
lived in the small house, last but one on your left,
as you go towards the windmill." A deep sigh
here. " You'll know it by wall-flowers growing at
the door; at least, there were, about a year or two
ago; and they had saved a little money; and Mr.
Foljambe had a very high opinion of them, and so
had I." The captain bows. " And about sixteen
years ago they gave up their house here, and went
to Coventry; it is a good way off, you know."

The captain knits his brows and calculates
rapidly.

"About forty-seven miles—by Jove, it *is* a good way."

"And when they arrived there, they set up a confectioner's shop, in a small way, of course."

"Oh?" says the captain, very much interested, "that was very spirited of them."

"It had a bow-window that was painted brown, it was at a corner of a street near one of the spires, and they did very well, and they are both alive still."

Another deep sigh followed.

"What a pity!" says the polite captain, who is looking across the table, and thinking, at the moment, of quite another thing. The good lady does not hear his comment, and so its slight incongruity is harmless, and the captain inviting the conclusion of the tale, says, "and——?"

But the story is over. That is all. And good Mrs. Foljambe, contented with her contribution towards keeping the conversation alive, is looking, in a melancholy reverie, on the table-cloth.

As she has dropped off his hands in this gentle way, the captain resigns her with a good grace, and listens, undisturbed, to other talk.

Lady Vernon has now taken the curate into council, and is leading the little cabinet. Mr. Michael Doody is attentive, and seems impressed by what Lady Vernon is saying. She has the reputation of being a clever woman, with a special talent for government.

Mr. Puntles is listening, and sipping his wine; and being a polite old man, now and then plagues Mrs. Foljambe with a question or a remark.

Doctor Malkin is in animated conversation with Miss Vernon. He is, perhaps, a little of an esprit fort; but in a rural region, always more pharisaical, as well as more pure than the city, he is very cautious, the more particularly as his great patroness, Lady Vernon, is a sharp and ready Christian, not high-church, not low-church; people at both sides of the controversy complain in whispers of ambiguities and inconsistencies; she is broad-church. Yes, very broad-church. She would throw the church-gates wide—as open as her heart—as open as her hand. She has built plain, sober churches — she has built meeting-houses—she has built florid chapels and churches, gleaming with purple and gold, and with saints and martyrs glowing in brilliant colours from stained windows, such as rejoice the heart of that learned and Gothic Christian, Archdeacon Complines. Her flatterers speak in this vein: and they are legion. The promoters of the projects which she vivifies by her magnificent bounty may hate their equally successful rivals, but they like her money;

and they are extremely careful not to offend her, for she has not the reputation of forgiving easily.

Doctor Malkin talks to Miss Vernon on her pet subjects, theories, and vagaries of all sorts, the abuses and corruptions begotten of an artificial system, bold social reforms, daring sentiments on all forms of civil government, treated romantically rather than very learnedly, or, indeed, very wisely.

And now Lady Vernon, having established an understanding with old Mrs. Foljambe, rises, and with that dejected lady, and Maud, takes her departure. Captain Bamme, gallantly standing as guard of honour, with the handle of the open door in his hand, smiles with supernatural sweetness, sees them off, and returns to complete the little party of five.

CHAPTER XVI.

A SKIRMISH.

PLUMP little Mr. Puntles is a cosey bachelor of two-and-sixty. Something of an antiquary, something of a herald, he is strong in county lore. He is the only man in Roydon who honestly likes books. He lives in the comfortable square brick house of Charles the First's date, at the northern end of the village. He usually takes a nap of five minutes after his dinner, and then is bright for all the evening after.

The Reverend Mr. Foljambe, who considers himself an aristocrat, talks with him upon genealogies, and such matters, with the condescending attention that befits his high descent and connexions.

"No family has a right to powdered-blue in their liveries, except this branch of the Vernons, one branch of the Lindseys, and two other families," said Mr. Puntles, with his eyes closed, and his finger tracing diagrams slowly on the table-cloth. "It is a very distinguished privilege, and I'll tell you how the Vernons came by it."

Mr. Foljambe smiles blandly, and also, nearly closing his eyes, inclines his ear; but a vociferation at another part of the table, where Captain Bamme and the curate were in hot debate, arrested the communication.

"Who consolidated your civil power in India?" urges the curate. "I'll tell you, captain. It was Mr. Richard Colley Wellesley of Dangan, in the county of Meath. The Marquis Wellesley, as you are good enough to call him. And who commanded the Indian army, at the same critical period, when something more was wanted than blundering and plundering, a teaste of genius and a teaste for thundering?"

Before answering his own question the Reverend Mr. Doody applied his glass to his lips, his disengaged hand being extended all the time toward his gallant adversary, with a paddling of the fingers, intended to retain the ear of the company and the right of continuing his speech.

"So far as thundering is concerned, Mr. Doody,"

said the vicar, with stately jocularity, "it seems to me that your countrymen seldom want a Jupiter."

The captain, with a rather inflamed visage, for more had passed between the curate and him, smirked angrily, and nodded at the vicar, and leaned back and tossed his head, and rolled a little in his chair, smiling scornfully along the cornice.

But the Reverend Mr. Doody could hear no one but himself, and think of no one but Captain Bamme and the Wellesley family at that moment, and he continued : " Who, I repeat, saved India by his genius for arms, as the other consolidated the same empire by his genius for organisation and rule? Who but that Irishman's Irish brother Arthur Wellesley, Jooke of Wellington? And I think I remember some trifling services that same county o' Meath man did you on other ground. But I'm speaking of India just now, and I ask again, who saved it, again, when its existence was imperilled by the natives? Who but my countryman, Irish Lord Gough, from Tipperary? It's easy for you, in quiet times, when you're enjoying the fruits of Irish gallantry and Irish genius, to make little of Ireland, but you know where to run for help when you're in danger."

"Haven't you a rather uncomfortable way of

putting it, Mr. Doody?" said the Reverend Mr. Foljambe, a little gravely.

"Why I can prove to you," began Mr. Doody, not hearing the vicar, "if you take up the old chronicles, that the Irish were in the habit of continually invading England."

"With what result?" inquired Mr. Foljambe, with a smile.

"Ship-loads of plundher and slaves," answered Mr. Doody, promptly.

"We had better look sharp," said cosey Mr. Puntles, who rather enjoyed the debate.

"If they had but a regiment of tall Irish clergymen, no doubt they'd march through the country," said the captain, laughing stingingly.

"If they had nothing but a regiment of small English captains before them," said the curate, "they'd do it easy enough. My dear friend," continued the curate, "I don't say, mind, that a mob can fight a trained army; but give us eighteen months to drill in, and see where you'll be; give us what ye must give us, before long, federalism, and before ten years, we'll conquer England!"

Captain Bamme uttered a short laugh of scorn.

"I hope you'll spare my little collection of curiosities," said Mr. Puntles, merrily.

"If you're strong be merciful," broke in Captain Bamme.

"Don't be frightened, captain; we'll spare them, and all other little curiosities too," said Mr. Doody, hilariously. "But, seriously, as sure as you're sitting there, Ireland will conquer England, if she gets a fair chance."

"That will be something new, won't it?" says the Reverend Mr. Foljambe. "Shakespeare says something about a country

> That never yet did lie
> Under the proud foot of a conqueror."

"Shakespeare said more than his prayers, sir; didn't he know as well as we do, that there is no country in Christendom that has been so often and so completely conquered as England? 'Did never lie!' ha, ha, ha! 'The proud foot of a conqueror?' Mighty fine! Did ye never lie undher the Romans? or the Saxons? or the Danes? or the Normans? and didn't they, one after the other, stay here and settle here, and take your houses and live in them, and your fields, and make ye dig, and sow, and reap, and stack for them? and didn't they drive you hither and thither, and tax ye, and work ye, and put ye to bed at sunset, and make ye put out your candles and fires by sound of bell? And after all, England did never lie under the proud foot of a conqueror! Sure, my dear sir, ye oughtn't to be talking like a madman. It's enough to make a pig laugh. Can't ye buy books, and read them?"

"But, sir, I'm very proud of those conquests," interposed Mr. Puntles, smiling happily. "All these invaders are blended down into one composite mass, and that fusion is the stuff that makes the modern Englishman."

"It won't do, sir; a few thousands scattered among millions never changed the blood or nature of a nation yet—you're Britons, still. You are Britons, the same as ever; by no means a warlike people, not gifted with any military aptitudes, pacific and thradesman-like, and the natural prey and possession of a nation with the spirit of conquest and a genius for arms. You're sinking into your natural, hereditary state, that of Quakers and weavers, contented with your comforts and your opulence, knuckling down to the strong, and bullying the helpless, and leaving soldiering in earnest to nations that have the heart and the head for that sort of game, and just taking your chance, and hoarding your money."

"Chance has answered pretty well up to this," said Mr. Foljambe; "we have escaped a military occupation tolerably well I hope."

"So has Iceland, sir, so has Greenland; ye're

out of the gangway, don't ye see, sir? I could show you in the middle ages——"

"Don't mind the middle ages," said the captain "pray don't—we won't undertake to follow you there."

"*You* won't follow me, captain, because ye're gone before me there, my dear fellow, ha, ha, ha!—ye're one of the middle ages of this place yourself, my dear captain; but never mind, age is honourable, and middle age is middling honourable, anyhow."

The captain stared hard at the decanter from which he filled his glass. He so obviously meditated a retort that the neutral powers interposed.

"Now, now, now—pray Captain Bamme take some wine, and send the decanters this way," said the vicar, who was in charge of the party; "and Mr. Doody, I think we have stood the Irish invasion very well, and I vote we declare an armistice and a—eh—what do you think?"

"We'll be better friends, captain, you and I," said Mr. Doody, generously, "when we come to understand one another; but don't ye be talking about things you don't understand. Stick to the cane and the pipeclay, my boy; and my blessing attend ye! and I pledge ye in a glass of clar't.

Gentlemen, I give ye our gallant friend Captain—— I give ye my word, I never heard your neeme. No matter; our gallant friend the captain; but I fill to ye all the same."

"I think he's gone." observed Doctor Malkin, rousing himself suddenly from a profound " brown study." So he was, although the Reverend Michael Doody, who, during his concluding remarks, had been staring at a claret jug, in the direction of which his powerful arm was extended. while he twiddled his fingers toward the handle, in general invitation to the company to push it within reach of his generous clutch, had not perceived his disdainful retreat.

" So he is! There now! Ye see what it is to be thin-skinned." said the curate, filling his glass and drinking it off. without insisting on the presence of the object of the compliment, or the participation of the rest of the company.

" That's good clar't. I'll trouble ye, sir, for the white wine—the madeira—thank ye, and I drink to our departed friend. the captain, and in solemn silence to the memory of his temper. the craiture !" Which ceremony. like the last. he had all to himself, and performed with a loud smack of his lips.

The Reverend Mr. Foljambe and Mr. Puntles

had dropped into their quiet feudal talk again.
Doctor Malkin would take no more wine, and the
tall and courtly vicar, having collected the general
suffrage in favour of joining the ladies, arose, and
the little party retreated, talking listlessly, in the
direction of the drawing-room.

CHAPTER XVII.

IN THE DRAWING-ROOM.

THE drawing-room is now in a blaze of wax-lights, and every object in it brilliantly defined. Miss Maximilla Medwyn has arrived, and stands near the fireplace, in a dark silk dress, with a good deal of handsome lace; otherwise the same erect figure, and energetic and pleasant face, that we have seen.

Two gentlemen have arrived to tea—a tall man, quiet and gentleman-like, of fifty years or upwards, who is talking to Lady Vernon, and a very short, vulgar man, fat and sleek-haired, with smooth chin and cheek, and ill-made, black, baggy clothes, and a general greasiness of hair, face, and habiliments. This is Mr. Zachary Smelt, a light in the firmament of Roydon dissent, who does not disdain to revolve, on occasions, round the munificent centre of so many religious charities, enterprises, and cliques.

Mr. Smelt has taught the muscles of his fat face to smile, with a perseverance that must have been immensely fatiguing when he first tried it ; but every fold and pucker in his cheeks was, by this time, as fixed as those of the great window curtains opposite to him were by the tacks and hammer of the upholsterer. I am sure he sleeps in that smile, and that he will die with it on. When he is angry it still sits on his putty face, though his little black eyes look never so fell and wicked over it.

" I'm less in the world, Mr. Smelt, than you are," Miss Maximilla is saying tartly enough to this good man, whom, instinctively, she loves not. " What do you mean by telling me I live too much in and for the world? You don't say that to Lady Vernon, I venture to say. You like her money too well to risk it. I venture to say you have fifty times as many spites, and a hundred times as many schemes, in your head as I. I have just as good a commission to speak plainly as you have. There's your great gun, the Honourable Bagge Muggridge, as you take care to advertise him whenever he attends a meeting, or makes a speech. He has gone out of the world, as you term it ; that is, he shirks his duties as a public man and a country gentleman, surrounds himself with parasites and flatterers, and indulges his taste for notoriety by making dull speeches at canting meetings, and putting himself down for shabby contributions to all sorts of useless things. And this selfish creature, because he gratifies his indolence and his vanity, and rides his hobby, has, you tell us, retired from the world, and become an apostle, and is perfectly certain of an eternal crown of glory. Those were your words, and I have seldom read anything more shocking."

Perhaps Miss Medwyn had something more to say, and no doubt Mr. Z. Smelt had somewhat to rejoin, for he was smiling hard, and folding and rubbing his fat hands together ; but the Reverend Mr. Foljambe walked slowly up with a gracious smile, his head inclined and his hand extended, and said, with dignified affection :

" And how is my very dear friend, Miss Medwyn ?"

The vicar chose not to see Mr. Smelt, though the shoulder of his fashionably cut clerical coat almost touched the forehead of that fat thunderer against episcopacy, whose fixed smile acquired under this affront a character as nearly that of a sneer as anything so celestial could wear. So Zachary Smelt, folding his fat hands, turned on his heel with an expression of malignant compassion, and Mr. Foljambe inclined his long face and high nose over Maximilla Medwyn, smiling, in his way, as sweetly as his fellow-labourer; and as his "very dear friend" answered his affectionate inquiries, his shrewd eye was peering after Lady Vernon, and I am afraid he could not have given a very accurate account of what the good old spinster answered.

A cloud crossed the pure light of his brow as he saw the fat dissenter, who was always extracting money for the behoof of his sect from Lady Vernon, place himself before her exactly as the tall grave man with the iron-grey head was withdrawing.

Mr. Foljambe turned out of his way, and looked into a book of prints which Doctor Malkin was turning over.

"An unexpected pleasure that," murmured the doctor, with smiling irony, as he glanced toward the short fat figure of Mr. Smelt.

"Oh! That is——?" hesitated the vicar, compressing his eyelids a little as he glanced towards Mr. Smelt, whom he knew as well as the doctor did. "I stupidly forgot my glasses."

"Mr. Zachary Smelt, the Independent preacher. I venture to say there is not a drawing-room in the country, except this, into which that fellow would be admitted," said the doctor, who had no practice among that sect.

"Well, you know, Lady Vernon may do things that other people couldn't. Smelt? Yes, he is a troublesome person, and certainly, I don't pretend to say—I don't stand, at all, I hope, on that sort of thing; but I should not suppose he can feel quite at home among gentlemen."

Doctor Malkin smiled and shrugged his shoulders.

"This is, you know, a very distinguished house," continues the vicar, loftily, "and not the place, as you say, where one would expect to meet people of a certain level in society; I don't object to it, though, of course, there are others who, I dare say, don't like it. But I do say it is a mistake, as respects the object of the distinction; it does not answer its purpose. I venture to say there is not a more uncomfortable man in this county to-night, than this Mr.—Mr.—a—Smelt."

"I'm not so sure; he is such an impudent fellow," said the doctor.

"I shouldn't wonder if he had a good deal of that kind of thing, as you say. You possibly have more opportunities than I can boast. You see, Doctor — a — Doctor — a — a — Malkin." The Reverend Mr. Foljambe had a habit of hesitating rather over the names of small men with whom he was good enough to converse. "Lady Vernon, though she is a church-woman, and a very staunch one, in a certain sense, has yet very vague views respecting the special sympathy due to those who, in a more intimate way, are of the household of faith; but she'll come all right, ultimately, with her powerful mind, and the supremacy she assigns to conscience in everything. I have had, from my position, opportunities, and I can safely say I have rarely encountered a mind so entirely under the guidance and control of conscience."

The Reverend Richard Howard Foljambe looked with the affectionate interest of a good pastor and kinsman at that paragon of women.

"What a splendidly handsome woman she is!" observed the doctor. "By Jove, for her time of life, she's perfectly wonderful."

Every one flatters Lady Vernon, and these gentlemen like to pay her compliments in each other's ears, though she does not hear them. This frank testimony behind backs prevents the least suspicion of adulation in what they may say in her hearing. But in truth, Doctor Malkin's criticism is no flattery, though, perhaps, they hardly know that it is not, their critical faculties being a little confused, standing so much as they do in the relation of courtiers to her.

They are both covertly looking at her. They see a lady of some four or five-and-forty, still very handsome, according to the excellence of middle-aged beauty. How refined and elegant she looks, as she talks gravely with that little vulgar dissenter. She is the representative of an ancient family. She is peculiar in appearance, in habits, in character. A fine figure, a little fuller than girlhood, but only a little. A Greek face, pale, proud, and very still.

"What a talent for command that woman has!" says the doctor.

"She's very clever—she's very able, I may say, is Lady Vernon," says the clergyman, who being a kinsman, does not quite like Doctor Malkin's calling her a woman.

"Did it ever strike you, sir, making allowance for the difference of sex, that her eye has a very powerful resemblance to that of a remarkable historic genius?" asks Doctor Malkin.

"Ah—well, I can't quite say; a—do you mean —I don't quite see," says the vicar.

"A large wonderful grey eye that will be famous as long as history lasts—I mean Napoleon the first consul, Napoleon the Great. It is powerfully like some of the portraits."

"Well, do you know, I should not wonder. I believe there is—very likely," replies the vicar.

"Now, Miss Maud's, you see, although they are large and grey, they haven't got that peculiar character—a look of serene command, and what some people would call cold; it is very fine."

"Yes, and accompanied with that talent, she has so much administrative ability! She is a Dorcas, but a Dorcas on a very princely scale indeed," says Mr. Foljambe.

"More like my idea of Minerva-glaucopis, you know—just that marble brow and pencilled eye-brow, and cold, full, splendid grey eye. It is a study for Pallas; it would be worth a fortune to some of our painters," says the doctor.

The doctor's face looks a little sterner as he closes his little speech. It is not always easy to say what a man is looking at with an obliquity of vision like his; but I think of his two rather fine dark eyes, that one which he chiefly uses glanced at that moment on Miss Maud Vernon. Perhaps some association or train of thought, suddenly suggested, caused the change. The doctor's face is well enough when he is talking and animated. In repose it is not prepossessing; disturbed by any unpleasant emotion it is still less so.

CHAPTER XVIII.

DRESSING-GOWNS AND SLIPPERS.

CAPTAIN BAMME, who has been entertaining the young lady, is taking his leave. The doctor says good-night at the same time, and walks down the old avenue in the long streak of moonlight between the shadows of the trees in company with the captain, who is eloquent upon the treason against the peace and decency of the town perpetrated by old Foljambe in the importation of his Irish curate.

"I hope I have a proper respect for everything that's sacred; but, by Jove, if a fellow behaves like a rowdy, parson or no parson, sooner or later, he'll get what he wants—a devilish good licking; and I'd chuck him out of the window as soon as look at him:" a feat not only morally but physically worthy of admiration, considering their relative proportions.

The curate meanwhile has taken his departure, and very amicably, side by side with Mr. Smelt, is trudging after the captain and the doctor to the village. These apostolic men are manifestly deep in conversation, if we may so call a talk in which the loud and hilarious voice of the curate, interspersed with his peals of laughter echoing among the branches of the ancient trees, does duty for both. The captain quickens his pace on hearing these ominous sounds. He was going to light his cigar, but does not care to loiter, and with a sniff and a muttered word or two between his teeth, postpones that indulgence till he shall have reached the gate, where, as he knows, the curate turns to the right, and he to the left.

Mr. and Mrs. Foljambe, in their one-horse brougham, come rolling down the avenue, and oblige the fat dissenter to skip out of the way as their wheel grazes his arm. He is, no doubt, grateful for his escape, but the fright does not abate his righteous abhorrence of prelatical pride; and the boisterous and unfeeling banter of the Reverend Michael Doody fails to soothe him as he stands gazing, for some seconds, after the equipage, with his muddy elbow a little raised. The driver and the parson are of one mind no doubt. If he had been a bishop would they have made his "lordship" cut that terrified caper? His blood boils as he looks after the carriage. The mud of the wheel, he could swear, is upon his shoulder. He half regrets, for the sake of the moral and the scandal, that he was not knocked down. Perhaps if he had possessed presence of mind he would have gone down at that touch, as adroit pugilists sometimes do in the ring.

Notwithstanding this little incident, however, Mr. Smelt and the curate proceed, side by side, in very friendly march toward the town.

The churchman's jocularity has subsided, and he is now learning all he can about the religious state of the little town of Roydon, and the statistics of its poverty, from the preacher at his side, who is puzzled a little by the unaffectedly secular demeanour of the curate, by his utter repudiation of the doctrine of apostolic succession, and by his earnest and simple desire to go to the heart of his work, and do some good in his generation.

From the cold moonlight, and still shadows of the foliage on the broad avenue, we return to the great drawing-room of Roydon and the glow of other lights, where the clear voice of Lady Vernon is saying to the tall, grey gentleman, with whom she has talked a good deal that evening, and who was on the point of going out to light his bedroom candle, and make his way to his room:

"I don't think I have introduced my daughter."

The tall gentleman's eyes follow the direction of Lady Vernon's expectantly, and she says:

"Maud, I want to introduce you to Mr. Coke, who has been so good as to come with the papers for the trustees, who are coming to-morrow, and it may be right that you should be present."

The elderly attorney looked at the young lady with interest as he made his bow, and he thought how high-spirited, how high-bred, and beautiful she looked, and what a becoming representative of that great and ancient family she was.

"It is a good many years since I saw you, Miss Vernon, a long time in your life, that is—not in mine. You were only so high," he says, with the familiarity of an old retainer, measuring a standard in the air with his hand.

Ten minutes later they have broken up and gone to their rooms, and Maud, in her dressing-gown, with her long hair loose over her shoulders, taps at her Cousin Max's door, which is near her own.

"Who's there?"

"Maud. May I come in?"

"Come in, my dear child, to be sure."

Maximilla Medwyn is in her dressing-gown and

slippers, and smiles—rather an odd figure, her dressing-gown being "skimpy," as her maid tells her often, and her head being made up in an eccentric coiffure.

"What is the matter now?"

"Nothing. Only I could not rest till I had seen you again. Mamma received me to-day just as usual."

"She can't help it," replies Miss Medwyn. "My maid is gone to her bed; there's no one to hear us. She is the same to every one: it is her way; she was always cold. I tried to know her long ago—and I believe she liked me as well as she liked any one else—but I never could know her, young as she was. It is her nature, and she can't change it now."

"I wish I could be cold and reasonable like other people. I wish I could care nothing about it, but—I'm such a fool."

"You make too much of it."

"I can't help it, and whenever I do speak out, we quarrel. It is so miserable."

"You must treat different people differently, my dear, according to their natures. I make it a point to meet her just as coolly as she meets me, and I find we get on very well," said Maximilla. "She was always an oddity. Why, nothing odder was ever heard of than her marriage with your

poor father. To me she always seemed unfathom-
able. All I know about her is, that she has the
strongest will I ever heard of, and that she looks
like a haughty lady superioress of a convent.
Very handsome, of course, we all see that; but
with a countenance, it seems to me, incapable of
sympathy, incapable of frankness, and dominated
by pride, and dead to everything else."

" You are frank enough, at all events," says the
young lady, a little dryly.

" Very frank always with you, Maud," replies
the old cousin, seating herself on the sofa at the
foot of her bed.

" I see more good in her than that," persists the
girl.

" So do I; but not in her face. She has a
great deal of good. She is generous; she is
courageous; she has many very fine points. But
she seems to me to hold every one on earth at
arm's length; that's all I say. As for me, I gave
up the idea of ever knowing her, twenty years ago.
You must take her for what she is, and be content
with so much love as she is capable of giving.
She may give more than she shows, for anything
we can tell, and I'm sure she'll do her duty. She
has always been a pattern of all the virtues."

" Yes, conscience, a strong sense of duty, every
one says that. I'm quite serious. But you said

that she was odd. What was there about her marriage with papa?"

"Well, yes, that was extremely odd. I never was so surprised in my life. Your father had his baronetage, but that in your family was less than nothing; that title had been twice offered within the last hundred years to the Vernons of Roydon, and twice refused. He was a handsome man, and rather agreeable, and there ended his attractions. He had not a guinea. He was twenty years older than she. He liked nothing that she liked. He was a captain in the Guards, you know, and when he was ruined, had retired. He came down here, and tried to make love to her, without your grandfather's knowing anything about it: but she could not endure him, and treated him with utter contempt, and he grew to hate her. People thought, my dear, that he did not want anything but her money, and was furious at finding himself foiled. She certainly did hate him, then. He was of the same family—a Vernon—her third cousin."

"Was not grandmamma alive then?"

"Yes, but in miserable health—slowly dying, in fact. They went away for a little tour, somewhere—a fancy of the doctor's, I believe: when she returned, which was in less than a year, your father came here, uninvited and unwished for. I was here at the time. Barbara seemed to hate him

more intensely than ever. She would not even
see him. She spoke of him to me, when I asked
her to come down and take her place as usual,
with a degree of detestation I could not understand."

"Yet he was very gentle, I have always heard,
and a great many people liked him," said Maud.

"I dare say. I only tell you what I saw," says
Maximilla. "I need not tell you I did not want
her to like him. I thought his courtship, all
things considered, a most audacious thing; and I
could not believe, after all that had passed, that he
had any serious idea of renewing it."

"It was certainly very unequal in all things but
birth," said Maud.

"Yes, you know, she might have married any
one, and he had no pretensions. Your grandfather
plainly did not like his being here, though he did
not choose to turn him out. I don't think, indeed,
he saw what Amyrald Vernon was aiming at; but
I could not help fancying that, for some reason,
he was afraid of him. Your grandfather was a
most upright, honourable man. If he had ever
been a reckless young man, or among objectionable
companions, I could have understood the possibility
of his dreading some awkward disclosure. But
his whole life had been transparent, and, in all
respects, honourable; and this puzzled me, for I

could not account for his seeming embarrassed and
timid in his own house, and so uneasy while
Amyrald Vernon continued there. I had given
up asking your mamma to appear as usual in her
place while he was there. One morning, however,
she did come down, hating him just as much as
ever, but thinking, I fancied, that it was making
him too important, keeping out of the way on his
account. I remember so well her standing for a
few minutes in the window, before breakfast, and
his joining her there, and talking to her. They
were both looking out, so I could not see their
faces. But the next thing that happened was
their taking a long walk, up and down the terrace,
together, after luncheon ; after that, her demeanour changed entirely ; he seemed to exercise an
unaccountable fascination over her ; and one
morning, in the drawing-room, she told me, as
coldly as if it was a matter of going to take a
drive, that she had made up her mind to marry
Sir Amyrald Vernon. I don't think I was ever
so astounded in all my life. I remonstrated and
represented all I could, but it was in vain ; whatever his fascination was, it had prevailed, and I
might as well have tried to lift the house from its
foundations by my eloquence. She must have
fallen in love with him. Her father always made
a pet of her ; too much, indeed. She would,

perhaps, under other management, have learned to be less wilful and less haughty. So, I suppose, he let her do as she pleased. But the end of it was that she did marry him ; and, I think, her liking, if there was any, expired before two months were over, for when I saw them next, she seemed—begging your pardon, my dear—to hate him as much as ever. They did not quarrel; I don't mean that. She was too cold and dignified for any such exhibitions. But I could not mistake her. There was fixed dislike. And when, two years later, he lost his life by the fall of his horse, I don't think she cried a single tear, and I never heard her speak of him, except now and then, as coolly and curtly as you might mention a not very pleasant acquaintance who had gone to Van Diemen's Land."

These recollections of Maximilla Medwyn's revived in Maud's mind a scene, which often recurred of itself.

It was one of those short scenes, in the remembrance of which fear and disgust are mingled; to disclosing which there grows up gradually an invincible repugnance, and on which the mind silently dwells with a sense of odious curiosity.

When she was a little thing, some five or six years of age, she was fond of old Margaret Creswell, who had been her mother's nurse. She used to run to her as a redresser of grievances, and to pour out her complaints and petitions at her knees. But a time came when her protectress was to take her last leave of her and of all things.

The old woman was dying, and found dying a hard and tedious piece of work. The child had not been in her room for four months, and one day, in a state of rebellion against some new rule of her mamma's, she broke from the nursery, and ran into old Margaret Creswell's room.

She was sitting up, in flannels, by the fire. The room was darkened. A little table, with her medicine bottles, her tablespoon, and glasses, was beside her. With her one idea the child trotted into the room, prattled and sobbed through her story, and ended by saying, "And that wouldn't be done to me if papa was alive."

The figure in the flannels beckoned, and for the first time, a little awe stole over the child; she drew near, trying to see her more distinctly in the obscurity. When she did, it was not the face she knew. There was no smile there. The face was hollow and yellow, a clammy blackness was about the lips, the eyes looked at her, large and earnest; the child came beside her, returning her strange gaze in silence. She was frightened that such a thing should be Maggie Creswell.

The old woman placed her bony hand on the

child's arm, and clasped it feebly. She spoke in a
hard whisper, with a little quick panting at every
word.

"That's Anne Holt has been saying that; it's
a shame to be putting things in your head against
your good mamma. Well it is for you that you
are under her, and not under him; no blacker
villain ever lived on earth than your papa. Keep
that to yourself; if you tell any one in the
nursery, I'll come to you after I'm dead, and
frighten you." She let go her arm, and said, "Go
now to your toys, and do as mamma bids you, and
be thankful."

Very much scared, and very quiet, the child
stole back to the nursery, and kept the secret
guarded by that menace.

That dark room; the old woman, stern and
changed; the last words she was ever to hear from
her; and the dreadful terms of hatred applied to
her father, which she tried to put away as a
blasphemy, returned often, and drew her into conjecture.

" Was there any reason," she asked her Cousin
Max, after a little silence, "for mamma's want of
affection for poor papa?"

" No particular reason—no good reason. As a
husband, I don't think there was anything against
him. He devoted himself very much to his duties,

and did his best to become a popular and useful country gentleman. I suppose she repented too late, and had acted on an impulse, and was disgusted to find, as many of us are, that the past is irrevocable."

Old Miss Maximilla sighed. Perhaps she had a retrospect to regret, and Maud, with the world before her, looked for a moment on the carpet sadly.

"I don't know your mamma, my dear; she has been always a sealed book to me. I don't think she ever wanted either sympathy or advice. I don't think any one ever knew her. *I* never could, and I have long given up the riddle. But, dear me, it is almost one o'clock. Run away, my dear, and let your poor old cousin get to her bed. I shan't go for a day or two, and we shall have time enough; I have fifty things to talk to you about. Good-night." And so they parted till next morning.

CHAPTER XIX.

BREAKFAST.

At half-past nine in the morning, the roar of the gong spreads shivering and swelling through rooms and passages, up staircases, great and small, through lobbies and long galleries, calling all the inmates of Roydon Hall to prayers.

In a long room which projects, at the end, in a mass of stone-shafted window, they assemble. A hundred years ago, and more, the then Vernon of Roydon gave to this great chamber, as nearly as he could, the character of a chapel. The light streams in through stained glass, brought from Antwerp tradition says, flaming from the base up to the cornice with sacred story. The oak carving of this sombre room is admired by critics, who say that the spoils of some ancient church must have furnished it. Mr. Coke, the elderly attorney, with his head full of the strategy of the consulting-room and the rhetoric of the courts, is for a moment solemnised, as he enters and looks round him. He then falls to admiring, in detail, the stained glass. He and Miss Max are the only guests at present in the house. It is a very small party confronting so imposing an array of servants. There is hardly another house in England where so prodigious a household assembles. Mr. Coke, whose business brings him, about settlements and at other legal crises, to many noble houses, is struck by the unusual superfluity of servant-kind here, and while Mr. Penrhyn, Lady Vernon's secretary, who officiates, when no clergyman is present, is reading a chapter from the Old Testament, he tries to count them, but his polling always breaks down in the middle, at the back rows; and then comes the thought, "Here are just one lady and her daughter, a girl, to be attended to, and this enormous piece of machinery is got up and main-tained, for that simple end;" and the words of "the preacher" stand good to this hour: "When goods increase, they are increased that eat them: and what good is there to the owners thereof, saving the beholding of them with their eyes?"

These morning prayers of Lady Vernon's are

unusually long. There are the psalms of the day, and the chapters, and, in fact, a "service," which lasts about half an hour.

Mr. Penrhyn has had his breakfast an hour ago, in his own little office, and having talked and smirked a little, remits himself, in a fuss, to his work.

The breakfast-room still bears the ancient title of the "parlour," and is a spacious and cheery apartment, hung with festive tapestry, and opening into the dining-room. Here the little party of four assembled.

"It is eleven years, Mr. Coke, I was counting up last night, since I last saw you; and I believe you are one of the very oldest friends I have," said Miss Max. "Why don't you pay me a visit at Wybourne, when your excursions carry you to points so near as Hammerton and Dake's Hall? I heard of you there. I don't think it was kind."

"It is all your fault," said Lady Vernon. "He went to Dake's Hall to arrange settlements. Why don't you give him a reason to visit you?"

"Thank you very much, Lady Vernon," put in Mr. Coke, merrily.

"I think it is rather hard that an old woman should be put into Coventry because she can't find any one to marry her," replied Miss Max.

"A lady who might have married any one of a

score of suitors, every one eligible, has no case to
make," Mr. Coke said.

"I think Cousin Max is right. I think one's
liberty is a great deal," remarked Maud. "Doctor
Malkin said last night what I quite agree in, that
it is better to marry never, than once too often."

"He says that a woman who marries once is a
fool," said Maximilla Medwyn; "but a woman
who marries twice is a criminal."

"Is not that rather violent doctrine?" Mr. Coke
inquired.

"I think he only said, who marries within a
short time after the death of her husband," said
Maud; "and you recollect the curious stories he
told us? There was a woman who would not
allow him to bleed her husband, whose life, he
said, would certainly have been saved by it, pre-
tending too great a tenderness for him to allow it,
and, in a few weeks after his death, she married a
person who lived in the house; and there was
another story of a woman who married immediately after her husband's death, without the
slightest suspicion, who, ten years later, was con-
victed of having murdered him, by hammering a
nail into his head while he was asleep."

"But, seriously, I'm a mere slave, and can
never command an hour, except when I get to
the Continent, and letters can't find me any

longer. Doctor Malkin was here last night? I
don't know the people—which was he?" said the
attorney.

"He is a pale man, with a high nose, and
dishevelled black whiskers, and good eyes," Miss
Maud answered.

"My dear Maud, that doesn't describe him,"
interposed Miss Max. "In the first place he
squints; next, he is bald, and he has a long upper-
lip and a short chin, and an odious smile, that I
think is both conceited and insincere, and you
could fancy him just the doctor, if he did not
like you, to bleed you to death, or poison you by
mistake."

"My dear Maximilla, how can you?" said Lady
Vernon, gravely, with a glow in both cheeks that
comes when she is either angry or otherwise
agitated. "My cousin, Mr. Coke, is not acquainted with Doctor Malkin. She does not
know him; but I do; and I have the very
highest opinion of him. I have great confidence
in his skill, and still greater in his integrity. He
is as conscientious a person as I ever met in my
life. I know no one more entirely trustworthy
than Doctor Malkin."

Lady Vernon spoke coldly after her wont, but
she was evidently in earnest.

"Then his countenance does him great wrong,"

answered Miss Max, cheerfully, "that's all I say. It is quite true I don't know him, and I don't desire to know him."

And she sipped her tea.

"I assure you, Mr. Coke, I speak from knowledge; there is no one of whose good sense and truth I have a higher opinion. I wished you to understand that," said Lady Vernon. "And I have an almost equally high opinion of his skill. For the last fifteen years he has been attending, in every illness, in this house; and he has been so attentive and so successful, it would be impossible not to have the highest opinion of him as a physician."

Perhaps Mr. Coke thought it a little odd that Lady Vernon should make such a point of his believing this country doctor a paragon; and wondered why the peculiar flush by which she betrayed excitement should glow in her cheeks, and make her broad, cold eyes, fiery.

"Country doctors are often the ablest," he remarked, letting the subject drop softly; "they get to know the idiosyncrasies of their small circle of patients so thoroughly; and their dispensaries and the rustic population furnish an immense field of observation and experience. Does Lord Verney come to-day?"

"Yes; I'm sorry he does, he is such a bore, poor man; I should have preferred his staying away," replied Lady Vernon, with plaintive disgust. "Barroden comes, and so does Mr. Hildering."

"And each, I think, brings his solicitor with him?" asked Mr. Coke.

"I wrote to them to do so, and I suppose they will," answered Lady Vernon. "Only Sir Harry Strafford doesn't come."

"I don't think we are likely to hit upon anything very new. I have gone over it so often, and I don't think anything has escaped us," ruminated Mr. Coke. "Is there a solicitor to represent Miss Maud Vernon?"

"No, I did not think it necessary. Does it strike you that this room is lighter than it was when you were last here?" inquired Lady Vernon, a little irrelevantly. "I'll show you how that happens."

And breakfast being by this time over, she rose and walked to the great window that looks towards the east. Mr. Coke, a little thoughtful, followed her mechanically.

"Two great lime-trees stood just there, where you see the grass a little yellow, and they were so shaken by the storm last year, that they were pronounced unsafe, and had to come down; they were beautiful trees, but the room is a great deal lighter."

"Yes," said Mr. Coke. "It is rather complicated, you see, and there might be a conflict of interests, and as the meeting is a little formal, it would have relieved me of a responsibility; but I'll do my best."

"I don't see that any conflict can arise. Mr. Coke," said Lady Vernon, coldly. "At all events, if she wishes to ascertain her rights and opportunities, or whatever they are, separately, there is nothing to prevent her. What we do to-day can't fetter her in any way, and I thought you were quite competent to protect us both. It would be rather early to anticipate her litigating with her mother. I should hope there won't be an opportunity."

"No," acquiesced Mr. Coke; "I should have preferred that arrangement; but I'll do my best. At what hour do you expect the trustees, Lady Vernon?"

"They will all be here by three o'clock, if they keep their appointments. I think Mr. Hildering will come at one; he said so."

Mr. Coke was thoughtful; and when Lady Vernon was gone, he looked over his note-book for a time, and raising his eyes a little after, he saw the slight figure of Miss Maximilla Medwyn walking up and down the long terrace before the house.

He went out and joined her.

CHAPTER XX.

LADY VERNON'S EXCURSIONS.

WHEN he overtook that cheerful sentry, he said : "Can you tell me where I should be likely to find Miss Vernon ? I have a word to say to her."

"Lady Vernon sent for her a few minutes ago, but she said she would not keep her long," said Miss Max; "I told her I should walk up and down here till she came."

Mr. Coke walked beside her without saying a word, till they had completed a walk to the end, and back again.

"Lady Vernon is as handsome as ever," he remarked, on a sudden. "Since I last saw her there is really no change that I can see."

" But that is scarcely a year ago," answered Miss Max.

" More than four," replied Mr. Coke, smiling.

" You mean to say you have not seen Barbara for four years!" exclaimed Miss Max, stopping short and turning towards him.

" I come whenever I'm sent for," said Mr. Coke, with a laugh. " But though I don't see her very often, I very often hear from her, and very clear and clever letters she writes upon business, I can tell you."

" But didn't you know she is in town for some time, every year of her life?"

" I had not an idea. We hear from her generally about once a fortnight. But I should very often have liked a few minutes' talk with her. Those little points of vivâ voce explanation are very useful in a long correspondence. And so she is every year at Grosvenor-square?"

" I think you had better not say a word about it to Lady Vernon," said Miss Max.

" Oh! of course not. I leave that to her. But I think it is a mistake, not giving us half an hour when she comes." Thus said Mr. Coke, swinging his stick a little, and looking over the top of the terrace balustrades, across the court, and ponds, and peacocks, and swans, and the close-shorn sward stained with the solemn shadows of the trees, down the perspective of foliage, to the mighty piers and great carved urns of the iron gates, and the gables and twisted chimneys of the gate-house.

"Yes, that would be only natural, and her not doing so puzzles me more and more," replied Maximilla Medwyn ; "you are such an old friend, and know everything about the affairs of this family so intimately, that I'll tell you ; but you are not to let it go further, for it is plain she does not want it talked about ; and it is simply that which makes me very curious."

"I've learned by this time to hold my tongue and to keep secrets, and I venture to say, this is a very harmless one," laughed Mr. Coke.

"Well, now, listen — what a time Maud is ! Once a year—I think about July or August—my handsome cousin, Lady Vernon, is taken with what my maid terms a fit of the fidgets. She takes her maid, but never Maud with her, mind— never. Maud has never come out. I don't think she has been six times in London in her life. That is not right, you know ; but that is a different matter. Lady Vernon and her maid go up to Grosvenor-square, where the house is all locked up and uncarpeted, all except a room or two, and where there is no one to receive them but an old housekeeper and a housemaid. She tells old Mr.

Foljambe, the vicar, that it is to consult a London physician. No great testimony, I think, to the surpassing skill of Doctor Malkin. But, I fancy, it is not about any such thing she goes to town, for her stay in Grosvenor-square never outlasts a day or two. Her fidgets continue. She leaves her maid there, and goes alone, I believe, from one watering-place to another."

"Without her maid, you say?"

"Yes, without her maid."

"And how do they know she goes to watering-places?"

"They never know where she is going. The only clue is, that now and then she sends a note of directions to her maid, in London, or to the house-steward, or the housekeeper, down here; and these indicate her capricious and feverish changes of place, which you'll allow contrast oddly with the stillness and monotony of her life, when she is at home. Then, after six weeks or so spent in this mysterious way, she appears again, suddenly, at her town-house, tells her maid that she is better, and so they return here. It is very whimsical. isn't it? Can you understand it?"

"Restlessness, and perhaps a longing for a little holiday," he answered. "She has, I may say, a very peculiar position in what they call the religious world; and the correspondence she directs, and even conducts with her own hand, is very large. Altogether, I think, she makes her life too laborious."

"Well, as you and she, and you and I, are all old friends, I don't mind telling you that I don't think that's it. I don't believe a word of it. There is more in it than that; but *what* I can't divine; and, indeed, it does not trouble me much; if Barbara would only do what she ought about Maud, I should be very well satisfied. But she has never been presented, nor been to town for a single season, and Lady Vernon has never taken her out, and I don't think has any idea of doing so. Of course, you'll say that, with all her advantages, it can't matter much. But there can be no advantage in people's saying that she has lived all her life like a recluse; and I think there is always a disadvantage in despising what is usual. And really, Mr. Coke, as a confidential friend, I think you might very well say a word about it."

He smiled, and shook his head.

"All that sort of thing is quite out of my line. But I think with you, it doesn't much matter: for she's the greatest heiress in England; and she is so beautiful, and—here's Miss Vernon at last."

As Maud came down the steps she looked to the right and left, and seeing Miss Max, smiled and nodded, and quickened her approach.

Mr. Coke advanced a step or two to meet her, with his business looks on.

" I have been wishing to say a word if you will allow me.   I think it would be advisable that you should be represented at the conference we are to hold to-day, to prevent any course being determined on that might embarrass your interests under the will; and if you authorise me to do so, I will watch them for you this afternoon; and, in any case, I'll mention that a solicitor should be retained for you, as the instrument is unusually complicated, and you will be of age in a very little time."

" I don't understand these things, Mr. Coke, but whatever mamma and you think right, I shall be very much obliged to you to do.   What a charming day it is!   I hope you are not to be shut up all day.   When you were last here it was winter, and you will hardly know the place now; you ought to see Rymmel's Hoe to-day, it is looking quite beautiful," said Miss Maud Vernon.

" I'm off, I'm afraid, to town this evening," he answered; " a thousand thanks.   I must now go in and see Lady Vernon, if she's at leisure."

So with a smile that quickly disappeared, he turned and walked up the steps.

CHAPTER XXI.

THE CONFERENCE.

OF this muster of trustees, Miss Maud Vernon gave this account in one of her long letters to her friend, Miss Mary Mainard:

"On Tuesday we had a little parliament of trustees, opened with great solemnity by mamma. She was aided by an attorney, a Mr. Coke, who says that your humble servant ought also to have been furnished with an adviser of the same profession. Old Lord Verney came similarly attended; and Lord Barroden also brought his attorney; Mr. Hildering, a great man in 'the City,' I am told, dispensed with that assistance, and, I suppose, relied on his native roguery. Still there was an imposing court of attorneys, sitting as assessors

with the more dignified members of the assembly.
Sir Harry Strafford, who is also a trustee named
in grandpapa's will, did not attend. As all these
were men of importance twenty years ago, when
they were named in his will, you may suppose
what a juvenile air the assembly presented.

"Mamma did not choose that I should attend,
telling me that I should be sent for, if required;
and I had begun to hope that my assistance had
been unanimously dispensed with, when a servant
came to tell me that mamma wished to see me in
the library. Thither I repaired, and found her
presiding at her cabinet.

"Lord Verney and Mr. Hildering were a little
red, and I fancy had been snubbing one another,
for Mr. Coke mentioned, afterwards, that they are
members of the same boards in London, and fight
like 'cat and dog' whenever they meet. Mamma
looked, as usual, serene, and old Lord Barroden
was, I am sure, asleep, for he was the only gentleman of the company who did not rise to receive
me. There were printed copies of grandpapa's
will, one of which was given to me; so I took a
chair beside mamma, and listened while they talked
in a language which I did not the least understand,
about what they called real and personal rever-
sions, contingent remainders, and vested remainders, and fees and tails, and more unintelligible

names and things than I could remember or reckon up in an hour.

"They all seemed to treat mamma with great deference; not complimentary, but real; and I remarked that they said very little across the table to one another; but whenever they had anything to ask or to say, they looked to her, and she seemed to understand everything about it, better than any one else in the room, and Mr. Coke told me, afterwards, she is one of the best lawyers he ever met, and he explained a great deal that I did not then understand.

"The conference lasted nearly three hours! You can't imagine anything so dull; and I came away just as wise as I went there, except, perhaps, that I had learned a little patience.

"The Rose and the Key, which, as you know, figure on our shield, were talked of a good deal, and are mentioned very often in the will, as indicating the families which are named particularly. Old Lord Barroden woke up at this part of the conversation, and talked a great deal of heraldry, whether good or bad I can't say; and then, as they were still very garrulous upon crests, supporters, shields, chevrons, and all the rest, mamma led the way to the state dining-room. I don't know why, we never dine there now; I think it about the prettiest room in the house—I don't think you saw

it, when you were with us. It has great stone
shields let into the wall all round, and ours over
the mantelpiece. They are all carved in relief, and
painted and gilded, according to heraldry; and you
can't think how stately and brilliant it looks. Old
Mr. Puntles, who is our antiquary in this part of
the world, says that it was an old English custom,
when a house was being built, for the owner to
place the arms of the principal families in the
county, thus, round the state dining-room, by way
of a compliment to them; and now I saw what I
never observed before, that in every second one, or
oftener, our device, the Rose and the Key, is
quartered in the corner. The rose, red; and the
key, gold; *gules* and *or*, they call them, on a field
azure : you see how learned I have grown."

Then the writer ran away to subjects more likely
to amuse her and her friend.

Mr. Coke did not stay to dinner. He took his
leave nearly three hours before that solemn meal.
As he came down-stairs from his room he encoun
tered Miss Vernon, who was going to dress.

"You are going to hear the bishop's sermon, and
see the statue unveiled?" he inquired, stopping
before her in the gallery.

"Yes, Miss Medwyn and I; mamma has a headache, and says she can't come," she replied.

"I'm afraid our long consultation tired her; I'm

sure it tired you, and I don't think you can have understood half we said. If you have five minutes, I'll describe to you now, just in outline, the leading provisions of your grandfather's will."

"I have more than five minutes, I'm sure," she answered; but not so much interested as Mr. Coke thought she might have been.

Young ladies are so much in the habit of being taken care of by others, that they can without much magnanimity dispense with the drudgery of taking care of themselves. They like whole bones as well as we do, but the vicious habit of being taken care of prevails, and what woman is quite capable of taking care of herself over a crossing?

"You must have for life, if you outlive your mother, Lady Vernon, at least ten thousand pounds a year, and you may have ultimately one hundred and fifty thousand pounds a year, in land, and a great deal of money beside—I don't think there is any lady of your age, in England, with such magnificent prospects. If Lady Vernon should marry, and have a son, the estates will go to him charged with ten thousand a year for you. If she should not marry, then, on her death, they go to you. If you marry, then your mother's power over the whole property will be very limited indeed. If neither you nor she should marry, then on your death the estates will go to some one to be appointed among certain families who are connected with yours, and who have a right to quarter the family device of the Rose and the Key."

"I've heard that before. Mr. Tintern of the Grange, near this, represents one of those families, I've been told?"

"Yes, and in that event, you or Lady Vernon, whichever survives, would have the right to appoint."

"I'm afraid, Mr. Coke, I have not mamma's talent for business. I should very soon be lost in the labyrinth."

"But, so far, you do understand?"

"Yes, I think I do."

"Well, there are also specific provisions in the event of your marriage, Miss Vernon, and perhaps, until you are furnished with a legal adviser, the best thing I can do for you will be to send you as short and simple an abstract of the will and its codicils as I can make out. The plan of the will is, to keep the estates together, and to favour certain families, out of whom, in the event of your both dying unmarried, an heir is to be appointed. If your mother marries, which I rather conjecture is by no means unlikely——"

He looked very archly as he said this, and some

complication of feeling made the young lady, though she smiled, turn pale.

" Do you really mean——?" began Miss Maud.

" I only say conjecture, mind, but I am generally a tolerably good conjuror, and we shall see. But, if Lady Vernon should marry," he continued, " her power over the estates is increased very considerably, but your reversion—I mean, your right of succession—cannot be affected by any event but the birth of a son. The provisions respecting the personal property—that is money, jewels, pictures, everything but the estates—are very stringent also, and follow very nearly the dispositions respecting the real estate. There is an unusual provision, also, with respect to all savings and accumulations, which may be made either by your mother, Lady Vernon, or by you, and they are to be carried to the account of the personal estate under the trusts; and very searching powers for the discovery of any such are vested in the trustees, and they are obliged from time to time to exercise them : and any such sum or sums, no matter how invested, are to be carried to the credit of the trustees to the uses of the will. So you see, it is a very potent instrument."

" I'm sure it is," said the young lady, with a disappointing cheerfulness.

" Well, I'll do my best; I'll send you an abstract;
and, is that the church-bell I hear?" he asked,
glancing through the open window.

" Yes, we hear it very distinctly," said she.

" Oh, then you'll be going immediately."

And again he took his leave.

CHAPTER XXII.

IN ROYDON CHURCH.

THE bell from the church tower sounds sweetly over town and field: and the sober-minded folk, who people the quaint streets of Roydon, answer that solemn invitation very kindly.

In this evening sun, as the parishioners troop slowly towards the church-gate, near the village tree, sad Mrs. Foljambe, hard of hearing, the gay Captain Bamme, and the new curate, the Reverend Michael Doody, accidentally encounter.

Mrs. Foljambe stops to receive their greetings. The level sunbeam shows all the tiny perplexity of wrinkles on her narrow forehead with a clear illumination.

"I'm going to the church to witness the ceremonial," shouts the captain, with his best smile.

She turns with a little start.

"No wonder she's a bit hard of hearing, captain, if that's the way ye've been talking at her this ten years," suggests Mr. Doody, in a tone to her inaudible.

"We have been sending up some china and cut-glass to the vestry-room, for the bishop's toilet-table," says Mrs. Foljambe, and her head droops, and her sad eyes look dreamily on the road, as if she were thinking of passing the rest of the evening there.

"The bell has only ten minutes more to ring, ma'am," says the curate, who is growing uneasy.

"It is a nice evening," observes Mrs. Foljambe, drearily.

"Quite so," says the captain, waving his hand agreeably towards the firmament. "Although we have sun, it's cool."

"Your son's at school?" repeats good Mrs. Foljambe, to let him know that she had heard him distinctly.

"Oh, oh, oh, that's rich!" ejaculates the curate, exploding.

The captain smiles, and darts a malignant glance at the Reverend Michael Doody, but does not choose to bawl a correction in the street.

So they resume their walk towards the church.
The sun is drawing towards the horizon; it is six
o'clock. The tombstones cast shadows eastward
on the grass, and the people, as they troop upward
toward the porch, throw their moving shadows
likewise along the green mantle of the dead, and
the grey churchyard wall catches them perpendicularly, by the heads and shoulders, and exhibits
in that yellow light the silhouettes of worthy
townsmen and their wives, and sharp outlines of
hats and bonnets, gliding onward, to the music of
the holy bell, to hear the good old bishop preach.

The bishop is robing in the vestry-room. The
vicar does the honours with profound suavity, and
the curate assists with a military sense of subordi-
nation and immense gravity.

A note awaits the bishop, in charge of the clerk,
from Lady Vernon, pleading her headache, and
begging the good prelate to come to Roydon Hall,
and if his arrangements about the Church Missions
meeting will not permit that, at least that on his
way back to the palace he will give her a day or
two, or as much longer a time as he can. One of
her grenadiers in blue and gold and cockade waits
at the vestry-door for an answer, looking super-
ciliously over the headstones. But the bishop
cannot accept these hospitable proffers.

In due time the statue is unveiled. In white

marble, the image of a slender man, of some forty
years or upward, with a noble pensive face, and
broad fine forehead, his head a little inclined,
stands forth, one hand laid lightly on an open
book, the other raised, in pleading or in blessing.
It is what we don't often see, a graceful, striking,
and pathetic monumental image.

Dead two-and-twenty years, there were many
present who remembered that energetic, charitable,
and eloquent vicar well.   And all who knew him
adjusted themselves to listen, with earnest ears, to
the words which were to fall from the lips of the
good old prelate, who preached, after so long an
interval, as it were the funeral sermon of his
gifted friend.

The Vernon family have a grand, old-fashioned,
square pew in the aisle; Maud Vernon and Miss
Max Medwyn sit there now, and the bishop's
chaplain has been, by special invitation, elevated
to its carpeted floor, and sits on its crimson
cushion, and performs his religious exercises on a
level at least twelve inches higher than the rest of
the congregation in the aisle.

Under the angle of the organ-loft, at each side,
is a narrow entrance.   And above that, at the
right, is a straight stone arch, separating the loft
from the side gallery, and looking diagonally

across the aisle. Behind this, going back deep
into the shade, is a narrow seat, with a door
opened by a latch-key from the winding tower-
stairs. Here you may sit between stone walls that
are panelled with oak, hearing and seeing, and
yourself unobserved. In old times, perhaps, it
was the private observatory of some ecclesiastical
dignitary or visitor, who looked in when he pleased,
secretly, to see that mass was sung, and all things
done decently and in order.

To those who look up, the arch seems empty,
and nothing but darkness in the cavity behind it.
But a human being in perturbation and bitterness
of soul is there. It is hard for her to follow the
benedictions of the psalm, to which the congregation read the responses that echo through the
old church walls. In the corner of the deep and
dark cell she occupies, there stands, as it were, an
evil spirit, and there ripples in and fills her ears,
with ebb and flow, the vengeful swell, but too
familiar to her soul, of another psalm—a psalm of
curses. Ever and anon, as if she would shake
something from her ears, she shakes her head,
saying :

"Is he not dead and gone? 'Vengeance is
mine, I will repay, saith the Lord.' Let him
alone. Don't think of him."

But the gall returns to her heart, and fire and worm are working there, and the anathema goes on.

Why had she committed it, syllable by syllable, with a malignant meaning, to memory, and conned it over, with an evil delight?

Had she abused the word of God; and was the spirit she had evoked her master now?

Though her lips were closed, she seemed to herself to be always repeating, fiercely:

"Set thou a wicked man over him, and let Satan stand at his right hand."

"When he shall be judged, let him be condemned: and let his prayer become sin."

"Let the iniquity of his fathers be remembered with the Lord; and let not the sin of his mother be blotted out."

"Because he remembered not mercy, so let it be far from him."

"As he loved cursing, so let it come unto him."

She raises her head suddenly.

"I'm nervous," she thinks, with her hands clasped over her dark eyes. "God have mercy on me, and let me hear!"

The voice of the good bishop, clear and old, is heard uttering the brief prayer before his sermon.

She throws herself on her knees, listening with

clasped hands, passionately. A dull life rolls away, and warm and vivid youth returns, and the fountain of her tears is opened, and the stream of remembrance, sweet and bitter, rushes in. The scene is unchanged, there is the same old church, there are the rude, familiar oak carvings, the self-same saints and martyrs in the vivid windows. The same sweet organ-pipes breathe through the arches from time to time the same tones to which, in summer evenings just like this, long ago, she had listened, when a loved hand pressed the notes, and the melancholy sounds filled her ears as they do now. Oh! the pain, how nearly insupportable, of scenes recalled too vividly, wanting the love that has made them dear to memory for ever.

Over the heads of the earnest and the inattentive, of dull and worthy townsfolk there assembled, the tremulous silvery tones of the white-haired bishop reach the solitary listener in this dark nook.

The old bishop tenderly enters on his labour of love. He eloquently celebrates his early friend. He tells them how gentle that friend was, how learned, how noble an enthusiast, modest and simple as a child, yet a man of the finest genius. Many of those who heard him now remembered Mr. Howard in the prime of manhood. Two-and-twenty years were numbered since his beloved friend died. They, too, were once young students together—it seemed but yesterday; and he, the survivor, was now an old man; and if the companion whom he had deplored, with foolish sorrow, were now living, he would be but the shadow of the man they remembered, with hair bleached, and furrowed brows, and strength changing fast to weakness. But time could not have changed the fine affections and noble nature that God had given him, and would have only improved the graces that grow with the life of the Spirit. Then follow traits of the character he described, and some passages, perhaps unconsciously pathetic, on the vanity of human sorrows, and the transitoriness of all that is splendid and beautiful in mortal man.

The feeble voice of the bishop is heard no more.

The organ peals, and voices skilled in the mystery of that sublime music rise in a funeral anthem: voices called together from distant places chant the magnificent and melancholy passages in Holy Writ that speak on the awful and plaintive theme of death.

Then in one long chord the voices faint and die, like a choir of angels receding from the earth. A silence follows, the organ peals once more, and the people begin slowly to disperse.

Old Mrs. Clink, who opens and locks the pews,

is waiting at the foot of the tower-stairs to receive Lady Vernon, whose brougham is to come to the church-door, when the people are gone, and there will be few to canvass the great lady's secret visit to the church.

The funereal swell of the organ still rolls and trembles along the roof, and fills the building, now nearly empty. The sun has just gone down; the fading mists of rose are still on the western sky. She ventures now to the front of the arch, in the shadow of which she has hitherto been hidden. The early twilight, dimmed by the stained windows, fills the church with a misleading and melancholy light; white shafts of marble rise faintly through the obscurity, and she, from her lonely place, unseen, looks down, crying silently as if her heart would break.

CHAPTER XXIII.

THE PARTY AT ROYDON HALL.

COLDLY handsome, an hour later, looked Lady Vernon, at the head of her table, with old Lord Verney beside her. Lord Barroden and her other guests, who had assisted at the legal consultation, were also of the party. The Dean of East Copely was there, very natty in his silk stockings, and apron, and buckles, and Sir Thomas Grummelston, Lady Grummelston, and Miss Grummelston, with several others who had attended the unveiling of the statue and the bishop's sermon.

Lady Vernon was never very gay; but she was this evening more than usually conversable and animated.

"What an admirable sermon the bishop gave us

to-day," remarked the Dean of East Copely. "He always preaches well, I need not say; but to-day there was so much feeling; it really was, even for him, an unusually fine sermon. Didn't it so strike you, Lord Verney?"

"I have had," said Lord Verney, looking across the table with his dull grey eyes solemnly upon the dean, "the advantage, Mr. Dean, of listening to the bishop of your diocese, in, as we say, another place. But I had been applying my mind to-day, I may say, to business a good deal, and although I have, people say, rather a facility of getting through business and things——"

Lord Verney's dull eyes at this moment had wandered to the bald head, flushed pink with champagne, of his attorney, Mr. Larkin, who instantaneously closed his eyes and shook his tall head with a mysterious smile, and murmured to the dean at his side:

"I wish I had his lordship's faculty; it would be an easy thousand a year in my pocket!" Which graceful little aside Lord Verney heard, and dropped his eyelids, raising his eyebrows with a slight clearing of his voice, and turning his face more directly towards the dean, suppressed in his own countenance, with an unusual pomp, a tendency to smile at the testimony of the man of business.

"People will form opinions and things, you know; and I was a little tired about it, and so I didn't mind, and I took a walk, and other people, no doubt, heard the bishop preach, and he seems to have gone somewhere."

"I wanted him to take his dinner here," said Lady Vernon, interpreting Lord Verney's rather vague but probable conjecture, "but he could not manage it."

"You were a little tired, also, I fear, Lady Vernon," said Mr. Foljambe. "A great many people, as well as I, were disappointed on missing Lady Vernon from her place."

"I had intended going, but I did feel a little tired; but I made an effort afterwards, though very late, and I glided into our little nook in the gallery without disturbing any one, and I heard the sermon, which I thought very good, and the anthem, which was better than I expected. I like our bishop so much; he's not the least a prig, he's not worldly, he is thoroughly simple—simple as a child; his simplicity is king-like; it is better, it is angelic. He is unconsciously the most dignified man one could imagine; and so kind. I have the greatest respect and affection for him."

"He was a good deal moved to-day," said Mr. Foljambe, leaning back a little grandly. "It is charming, so much sensibility; I saw him shed tears to-day while he spoke of the early years of Mr. Howard, my predecessor."

Mr. Foljambe blinked a little, as he said this, being always moved by the tears of people of any considerable rank, hereditary or otherwise.

Lord Verney being thus addressed by the stately vicar, whom he assumed to be a man of some mark, made answer a little elaborately.

"Sensibility and all that, I think, very well in its place; but in public speaking—and I hope I have had some little experience, I ought—sensibility, and that kind of very creditable feeling, ought to be managed; there's a way of putting up the pocket-handkerchief about it—all our best speakers do it—to the face, because then, if there *are* tears, and things, the faces they make are so distressing, and you see, by means of that, it is always managed; I can do it, you can do it, any one may do it, and that is the way it is prevented."

"Very true," said Mr. Foljambe, thoughtfully nodding, as he helped himself to a new entrée, a something aux truffes, which piqued his curiosity; "one learns something every day one lives."

"You don't, of course, recollect Mr. Howard very distinctly, Lady Vernon?" inquired the Dean of East Copely.

"Perfectly—I was past twenty when he died."

"A plain man, I should say, judging from that statue?" inferred the dean.

"He was not that—no—he had a very agreeable countenance, and his features were well-formed—his forehead particularly fine," she replied.

"His opinions were, I've been told, very unsettled indeed," said the dean.

"It did not appear from his preaching, then. It was admired and approved, and the then bishop was not a man to permit any trifling with doctrine, any more than the present," answered Lady Vernon. "Mr. Howard was very much beloved, and a most able teacher—his influence was extraordinary in this parish—I am speaking, of course, upon hearsay a good deal, for at that time I did not attend as much as I ought to such things, and my father was still living."

"Mr. Howard was, I believe, very highly connected?" said the dean.

"Quite so," answered Mr. Foljambe. "In fact, as far back as we can go, there was Chevenix, and then Craven, and Vernon, one of this house; and then Percy, one of the old Percys, and Dormer, and Stanley, and Bulkely, and Howard; and, in fact, it is really quite curious!—the people here do seem always to have liked to be taken care of by gentlemen," said Mr. Foljambe, grandly.

"I can't see that there is anything very curious

in that," said Lord Verney. "I can't concede that. One naturally asks oneself the question, why should not a gentleman be preferred? And one answers, he should be preferred, because he is naturally superior to persons who are inferior to him ; and we know he has certain principles and things that all gentlemen have, about it, and that, I conjecture, will always account for gentlemen, and things, being considered in that sort of light."

"I entirely concur," said Mr. Foljambe, who always concurred with peers. "I only meant that it is a little curious that the vicarage of Roydon should have been always filled by a person of that stamp."

"That is what I have been, I hope, endeavouring to say, or, rather, what I have not said, because I have endeavoured to say something different ; in fact, that it is *not* curious. I'll take some sherry about it." The concluding remark was addressed to the butler.

And so the conversation proceeded very agreeably.

But—

> Pleasures are like poppies spread,
> You pluck the flower, its bloom is shed.

The most agreeable dinner-party, its cutlets and conversation, its wit and its wines, are transitory,

and the hour inevitably arrives when people prefer
their night-caps, and the extinguisher.

Lord Verney has uttered his last wise and lucid
exposition for the evening, and the stately vicar,
who would not object to a visit to Lord Verney's
hospitable house at Ware, has imbibed his latest
draughts from that fountain of illumination. Lord
Barroden has said his say to Lady Vernon, and
enlivened by a nap, has made some agreeable
sallies in conversation with Lady Grummelston;
and to that happy lady, in the drawing-room,
Mrs. Foljambe has told her story about the two
young women in whom she took an interest, who
left Roydon and set up a confectioner's shop in
Coventry, and prospered.

The pleasures of that festive evening are over;
and Miss Max and Miss Vernon are having their
little chat together, in their dressing-gowns.

Miss Max has a little bit of fire in her grate, for
this is, thanks to our variable climate, by no means
like last night; not at all sultry, rather chilly, on
the contrary.

"Well, we shall soon hear something, I fancy,
about mamma's annual trip to town," says Maud,
speaking from a very low-cushioned chair in a
corner of which she is nestled, with her feet on the
fender.

The young lady's dressing-gown is of rose-coloured cashmere, some of the quilted silk lining of which, in her careless pose, appears. She is extremely pretty, looking up from her cushioned nook at the old lady, who sits, in her odd garb, before the fire in a more formal arm-chair.

" And why do you think so? Have you heard anything?" asks the old lady.

" Only that Jones says that Latimer is making the usual preparations," answers Miss Maud.

" Latimer's her maid, I suppose?"

" Yes."

" And why dosen't she ask Latimer directly?" demanded Miss Max.

" Because Latimer would be afraid to tell, and *she* would be afraid to ask. Mamma finds out everything she chooses to find out. You don't know mamma as well as I do in this house. Whatever she chooses to be secret is secret, and whatever she chooses to know she does know; and the servants are awfully afraid of her. You might as well ask that picture as Latimer; and Jones would not be such a fool as to ask her, for she does not know the moment mamma might say, ' Latimer, has any one been asking you anything about my going to London?' and so sure as she did, Latimer would tell her the truth, for there is no fault she is so summary upon as a falsehood:

and the servants think that she somehow knows everything."

"Well, at all events, Jones thinks she is going in a week?" says Miss Max.

"Yes. Do you know what Mr. Coke said to me to-day?"

"No. What?" says Miss Max, looking drowsily into the fire.

"He said he thought, or had reason to think, or something of that kind, that mamma is going to marry."

Miss Max turned, with a start, and looked for a few silent moments at Maud.

"Are you sure?"

"Perfectly sure."

"Well, that is very odd. Do you know, I've been thinking that, this long time. Did he say why he thought so?"

"No."

"Nor who the person is?"

"No; nothing. He only said that, and he looked very sly and mysterious."

"Mr. Coke is a very shrewd man. I don't think he had heard before of your mamma's excursions, and when I told him to-day I saw that his mind was working on what I said, and I suspect he has connected something he may have learned from a different source with what I told him, and has put the whole case together, and formed his conclusions. I wonder you did not make him tell you all he knew. I wish he had said so much to me. I should have made him say a great deal more, I promise you."

"He talks to me as if I were a child, and it came so much by surprise, and really I don't think I could have asked him one word about it; I felt so insulted somehow, and disgusted."

"Suppose she has fallen in love with some one of whom, for some reason or other, she is a little ashamed, and suppose there is an engagement? I don't understand it. I have been suspecting something for some time, and I did not like to say so, but you see it has struck Mr. Coke the same way. If it is that, there is a disparity of some kind you may be sure."

"I dare say. I don't care," says the young lady, who looks, nevertheless, as if she did care very much. "I shall have as much money as I want. Mr. Coke said I should have ten thousand a year, and I should go and live with you. You would take me in. Here nothing on earth should induce me to remain. She merely took a fancy to papa, soon grew tired of him, and ended by disliking him. But I shan't stay here to see his place filled and his memory insulted, and to be hectored and ordered about by some low man."

"I shall be only too glad to have you at any
time as long as you will stay with me.   But don't
be in too great a hurry.   You are assuming a great
deal; and even if she does marry, it may turn out
very differently; and you know, my dear, widows
will marry without intending any particular affront
to the memory of their first husbands."

"It is not a pleasant home to me as it is," says
the young lady, glancing fiercely along the hearth;
"but if this takes place I shan't stay here to see
it; that I am resolved on."

"In about a week she'll go, Jones thinks?" asks
Miss Max.   "I have grown very curious.   I should
like to see what sort of swain she has chosen.   You
never know what fancy a woman may take.   He
may be a very third-rate man.   I was thinking he
may possibly be in the army.   Mrs. Stonix swears
she saw her alone in Chatham last year.   But it is
growing awfully late.   Good-night.   We'll get to
our beds and dream it over."

CHAPTER XXIV.

A GENTLEMAN IN BLACK.

THEY had both risen preparatory to Miss Maud's flitting and a parting kiss and good-night, when Miss Max said, suddenly :

" And what about Mr. Marston ?"

" Well, what about him?" answered Miss Vernon, a little crossly, for she had not recovered the conversation that had just occurred.

" Nothing very particular—nothing at all, in fact—only I had intended talking about him fifty times to-day, and something always prevented. He's coming to the ball at Wymering, isn't he ?"

" I don't know ; he said so. I don't care," said

the handsome girl, drowsily. And she advanced her hand and her lips a little, as if for her final salutation.

But Miss Max had not quite done.

"I like him so much. I think him so clever, and so good-natured, and so nice. I wish so much, Maud, that you and he were married," said Miss Max, with audacious directness.

"And I wish so much that you and he were married," retorted Maud, looking lazily at the flame of her bedroom candle, which she held in her hand. "That would be a more natural consequence, I think, of your liking and admiring."

"You can't deny that he is wildly in love with you," said Miss Max.

"I can't deny that he was perhaps wildly in love with a poor seamstress in a dark serge dress a few days ago, and may possibly be in love with another to-day. That is wildly in love, as you say. I don't think there is anything very flattering in being the object of that kind of folly."

"Well, he will be a good deal surprised, I venture to say, when he comes in quest of his seamstress to the Wymering cloak-room," remarked Miss Max, with a pleasant anticipation of the éclaircissement.

"That depends on two things: first, how his seamstress meets him; and secondly, whether she meets him there at all. Good-night. It is very late."

And with these words she kissed her genial old friend, and was gone.

Miss Max looked after her, and shook her head with a smile.

"There goes impracticability itself!" she says, and throws up her hands and eyes with a shrug. "I pity that poor young man; Heaven only knows what's in store for him. I shall engage in no more vagaries at all events. What an old fool I was to join in that madcap project of rambling over the country and concealing our names! What will Mr. Marston think of us?"

When she laid her busy, rheumatic little head, bound up in its queer night-cap, on her pillow, it began at once to construct all manner of situations and pictures.

Here was a romance in a delightful state of confusion! On this case her head may work all night long, for a year, without a chance of exhausting its fertile problems; for it presents what the doctors call a complication. Barbara Vernon, with her whole heart, hates the Warhamptons; and the Warhamptons, with all theirs, detest Barbara Vernon. It is too long a story to tell all the aggressions and reprisals which have carried the feud to the internecine point.

"I must certainly tell Maud. I'll tell her in the morning," thought Miss Max. "It's only fair."

Perhaps this incorrigible old matchmaker fancied that it might not prejudice Mr. Marston if Maud knew that her mother had placed him under anathema.

By noon next day Lord Verney and Lord Barroden, and their attorneys, had taken flight, and Miss Maximilla Medwyn had gone on to see friends at Naunton, with an uncertain promise of returning in a day or two to Roydon Hall.

There is no life in that grand house but the phantom life on its pictured walls, and the gliding life of its silent servants. The hour is dull for Maud, who sits listlessly looking from one of the great drawing-room windows. Lady Vernon, who has seen, in succession, two deputations in the library, returns, and in stately silence sits down and resumes her examination of a series of letters from the late Bishop of Rotherham, and notes them for transmission to Mr. Coke.

Maud changes her posture, and glances at her mother. Why is there never any love in the cold elegance of that face? Why can't she make up her mind and be patient? The throb of life will as soon visit that marble statue of Joan of Arc, by the door; Psyche at the other side, in her chill beauty, will as easily glow and soften into flesh.

Miss Vernon leans on her hand, listless, gloomy —in a degree indignant.

The room is darkening. The darker the better, she thinks. It is no metaphoric, but a real darkness; for clouds portending thunder, or heavy rain or hail, have, on a sudden, overcast the sky, and are growing thicker.

The light is dying out, the shadow blackens on Lady Vernon's letters; she raises her eyes. One can hardly see to read.

Lady Vernon lays her letter on the table. She can no longer see the features of the Titian over the door, and the marble statues at either side have faded into vague white drifts. Some heavy, perpendicular drops fall, plashing on the smooth flags outside the window, and the melancholy rumble of distant thunder-booms, followed by a momentarily aggravated down-pour, and a sudden thickening of the darkness.

This was a rather sublime prelude to the footman's voice, announcing :

"Mr. Dawe."

Maud glanced toward the door, which was in obscurity, and then at Lady Vernon, who, sitting full in the light of the window, had turned, with a stare and a frown, as if she had heard something incredible and unwelcome, toward the person who was entering.

By no means an heroic figure, nor worthy of being heralded by thunder, has stepped in somewhat slowly and stiffly, and halts in the dim sidelight of the window, relieved by the dark background. It is a small man, dark visaged, with a black wig, a grave, dull, mahogany face, furrowed with lines of reserve. Maud is certain that she never saw that small, insignificant-looking man before, who is staring with a very grave but not unfriendly countenance at her mother.

He is buttoned up in a black outside coat, with a cape to it; he holds a rather low-crowned hat in his hand, and wears those shining leather coverings for the legs, which are buckled up to the knees. Getting in and getting out of his posting carriage he has scrupulously avoided dust or mud. His boots are without a speck. His queer hat is nattily brushed, and, in stable phraseology, has not a hair turned. His black coat is the finest possible, but it has great pockets at either side, each of which seems laden with papers, mufflers, and other things, so that his hips seem to descend gradually, and culminate near his knees.

This man's brown face, smoothly shaved, is furrowed and solemn enough for five-and-sixty. In his dress and air there is nothing of the careless

queerness of a country gentleman. His singularities suggest rather the eccentricity of a precise and
rich old city humorist.

There is something characteristic and queer
enough, in the buttoned-up and black-wigged little
man, to interest Maud's curiosity.

He has not been ten seconds in the room, and
stands poised on his leather-cased legs, looking
gravely and quietly at Lady Vernon, and, like a
ghost, says nothing till he is spoken to. One can
reckon the tick, tick, tick of the Louis Quatorze
clock on the bracket by the chimney-piece.

Lady Vernon stood up with an effort, still looking hard at him, and advancing a step, she said:

"Mr. Dawe? I'm so surprised. I could scarcely
believe my ears. It is such an age since I have
seen you here."

And she put out her hand hospitably, and he
took it in his brown old fingers, with the stiffness
of a mummy, and as he shook it slightly, he said in
his wooden tones, quietly:

"Yes it is. I was looking into my notes yesterday—it *is* a good while. You look well, Barbara.
Your looks are not much altered; no—considering."

"It is very good of you to come to see me: you
mustn't stay away so long again," she replied in
her silvery tones.

"This is your daughter?" he interrupted with a

little wave of his dark, thin hand towards the young lady.

"Yes, that is she. Maud, shake hands with Mr. Dawe."

"Maud Guendoline she was baptised," he said. as he advanced two stiff steps toward her, with his prominent brown eyes fixed upon her. She rose and placed her pretty fingers on that hand of box-wood, which closed on them.

CHAPTER XXV.

THE COUNTY PAPER.

WHEN he had inspected her features for a time, he turned to her mother and spoke.

"Not like her father," he said, still holding her hand.

"Don't you think so?" answered Lady Vernon, coldly. "I can see a look—very decidedly."

Maud was wondering all this time who this Mr. Dawe could be, who seemed to assert a sort of dry intimacy with Lady Vernon and her family, very unusual in the girl's experience.

"I think it is more than a look. I think her extremely like him," insisted Lady Vernon, resuming in the same cold tone, and without looking at

Maud, as if she had that resemblance by heart, and did not like it.

"She has some of the family beauty, wherever she got it," said Mr. Dawe, deliberately, in his hard quiet tones, and he let go her hand and turned away his inflexible face and brown eyes, a good deal to the young lady's relief.

Lady Vernon was still standing. She did not usually receive such guests standing. There was a hectic red in each cheek, also unusual, except when she was angry, and she had not been angry.

"Her eyes resemble yours," said Mr. Dawe.

"Oh, no. Perhaps, indeed, the colour; but mere colour is not a resemblance," answered Lady Vernon, with a cold little laugh, that, in Maud's ear, rang with cruelty and disdain. "No, Maud's good looks are all her own. She doesn't, I think, resemble me in any one particular—not the least."

Maud was wounded. She felt that tears were rising to her eyes. But her pride suppressed them.

"H'm!" Mr. Dawe hummed with closed lips.

"Of course, Mr. Dawe, you are come to stay a little? It is so long since you have been here."

"I'm not so sure about staying. It is a long time—sixteen years and upwards. You have been well; you have been spared, and your daughter, and I. We have all reason to be grateful to the

Almighty. Time is so important, and eternity so long!"

"Very true," she said, with a deep sigh, "and death so irremediable."

Mr. Dawe took his big silver snuff-box from his coat-pocket, and tapped it. He nodded, in acquiescence in the sentiment, leaned a little forward, and took a large pinch, twiddling his fingers afterwards, to get rid of any snuff that might remain on their tips. Perhaps the little superfluous shower that fell to the carpet suggested unconsciously his funeral commentary.

"Ay, dust to dust."

Whereupon he applied his Indian silk handkerchief, not to his eyes, but lightly to his nose.

"By-and-bye I shall have a word to say to you," he said, with a solemn roll of his brown eyes.

She looked hard at him, though with a half-flinching gaze, as if to read the character of his news. But the solemn reserve of his wooden face never changed.

"We shall be quite to ourselves in the library," she said.

"Then suppose we go there now."

"Very well; let us go," she said, and led the way.

At the door he made, with his stiff backbone, a little inclination to Miss Maud.

The door closes, and the young lady is left to herself, with matter for speculation to amuse her.

Quite alone in that vast and magnificent room, she looks wearily round. The care of Mr. Tarpey, on whom devolves the arrangement of flowers and of newspapers, has spread a table in a corner near the window with these latter luxuries.

Maud looks out; the rain is still tumbling continuously, and plashing heavily, though the sky looks lighter. She turns her eyes on the newspapers, and goes over to the table, and looks down upon them with listless eyes.

She carelessly plucks the county paper from among its companions, and in that garrulous and homely broad-sheet a paragraph catches her suddenly earnest eye. She reads it twice. The annual Wymering ball is to come off three weeks earlier than usual. She takes the paper to the window and reads it again. There is no mistake about it. "Three weeks earlier than the accustomed day!" There is an unusual colour in her cheeks, and a lustre in her eyes. She fancies, as she muses, that she hears a step in the passage, and she drops the paper. She is afraid of Lady Vernon's all-seeing gaze. and the dreadful question, "Have you seen anything unusual in the paper? Allow me to look at it." And she feels that her face would proclaim, to all who cared to look, that the Wymering ball was to take place three weeks earlier than usual.

No one is coming, however. She hastens to replace the paper on the table, and she sits down, with a pretty flush, determined to think.

She does not think very logically, or very much in train, and the effort subsides in a reverie.

Well, what is to be done now? The crisis has taken her by surprise; then fancy leads her into the assembly-room at Wymering. There are lights, and fiddles, and—oh, such a strange meeting!

Cousin Max must be with her. With that spirited veteran by her side she would fear nothing.

Very glad she was when one of Lady Vernon's broughams drove up to the door a few minutes later.

In that great house you cannot get as quickly to the hall as, on occasions like this, you may wish. But Maud overtakes her at the foot of the stairs, as in her cloak and bonnet Maximilla Medwyn is about to ascend to her own room.

"Mamma is in the library; and there are three men, with ill-made clothes and lank hair, a deputation, as usual, waiting in the shield-room to talk to her about a meeting-house at Heppsborough; and two clergymen are waiting in the blue drawing-room, to see her afterwards about plate for the church of Saint Hilary. So you and I shall be

very much to ourselves for a time; and do you
know we have had a new arrival—a guest. I
dare say you know him. Such an odd little
figure, as solemn as a conjurer. His name is
Dawe."

"Dawe? Why, for goodness sake, has Richard
Dawe appeared again?" exclaims Miss Max, stopping on the stair, and leaning with her back
against the massive banister in great surprise.

"His name is certainly Dawe, and I'll tell you
what he's like."

And forthwith Maud describes him.

"Oh! there's no mistaking the picture," cries
Miss Max; and then she is taken with a fit of
laughing, very mysterious to Miss Maud.

Recovering a little, she continues:

"Mr. Dawe? We were very good friends. I
like him—at least, all I could ever know of him in
twenty years. He keeps his thoughts to himself
a good deal. I don't think any one else in the
world had half his influence with your poor
grandpapa; but, certainly, I never expected to
see him here during Barbara's reign. My dear!
I thought she hated him. He was the only person
who used to tell her, and in the simplest language,
what he thought of her. Have they been fighting
yet?"

"No, I think not—that is, they had not time. I don't know I'm sure what may be going on now."

"Where are they?"

"In the library," says Maud.

"I think he is the only person on earth she ever was the least afraid of. I wonder what he can have to say or do here. He has never been inside this door since—yes, he did come once, for a day or two, a few years after your poor papa's death, and that, I think, was simply because he had some direction of your grandfather's, about the Roydon vault, which he had promised to see carried out; but, except then, he has never once been here, till now, since your poor grandpapa's death."

"How did he come to have such an influence here?" asked Maud.

They had resumed their ascent, and were walking up the stairs, side by side.

"I believe he understands business very well," and he is, I fancy, the best keeper of a secret on earth. His influence with your grandpapa increased immensely toward the close of his life; and he knew he could talk to him safely about that wonderful will of his."

"I wonder he allowed him to make that troublesome will," said Maud.

Miss Max laughed.

"I said the very same thing to him once, and he answered that he could not dissuade him, but that he had prevented a great deal. So, here we are."

The latter exclamation accompanied her entrance into her room.

Maud was more curious than ever.

"He's not the kind of person, then, who would have come here, under all the circumstances, without good reason," she said.

"Not he. He has a reason—a strong one, you may be very sure of that. It is very odd. I can't imagine what it can possibly be about. Well, leave him to me. I think he's franker with me than with any one else; and I'll get it from him, one way or other, before he goes. You'll see."

In this sanguine mood Miss Maximilla Medwyn put off her things, and prepared very happily for luncheon.

Mr. Dawe and Lady Vernon are, in the mean time, holding a rather singular conference.

CHAPTER XXVI.

COLLOQUY.

ON reaching the library, Lady Vernon touched the bell.

"You know this room very well, Mr. Dawe? You see no change here?"

"This house has seen many generations," said he, looking up to the cornice and round, "and will see out a good many generations more."

He steps backward two or three steps, looks up at the Vandyck over the mantelpiece, nods to that very old acquaintance, and says "Yes."

Then he rolls his prominent eyes again about the room, unusually shadowy on this dark day, and spying a marble bust between two windows, the little man walks solemnly towards it.

"That is Mr. Howard, who was our vicar, long ago," says Lady Vernon.

The blue livery is standing, by this time, at the opened door.

"Poor papa placed that bust there," she continues, "and it has remained ever since."

"Indeed!" says Mr. Dawe, and peers at it, nose to nose, for some seconds.

"They took casts from it," she continues, "for the statue that the bishop wished to place to his memory in the church."

"*Here?*" says Mr. Dawe, turning his profile, and rolling his brown eyes suddenly on her.

"Yes, in the church of Roydon, of course, where, as vicar, he preached for so long."

"I see," says Mr. Dawe.

"I shall be engaged for some time, particularly, on business," says Lady Vernon to her footman, "and you are to admit no one."

"Yes, my lady."

And the apparition of gold, azure, and powder (for they still wore powder then) steps backward, the door closes, and they are alone.

Lady Vernon is smiling, with bright hectic patches in her cheeks. There is something a little piteous and deprecatory in her smile.

"We are quite alone now. Tell me what it is,

she says, in a voice that could have been scarcely heard at the door.

Mr. Dawe turns on his heel, walks briskly up, and seats himself near her. He takes out his old silver box, with groups of Dutch figures embossed on it, and takes a pinch of snuff preparatory, with his solemn eyes fixed on her.

"Is it anything—alarming—what is it?" she almost gasps.

"There has been illness," he says, with his unsearchable brown eyes still fixed on her.

"Oh, my God! Is he gone?" she says, turning as white as the marble Mr. Dawe has just been looking at.

"Captain Vivian has been very ill, yes, Elwyn has been very dangerously ill," says the imperturbable little man in the black wig; "but he's out of danger now, quite—that's all over."

There was a silence, and Lady Vernon was trembling very much. She placed her finger-tips hard against her forehead, and did not speak for a few minutes.

Mr. Dawe looked at her with stoical gravity, and taking his spectacles from a very shabby case, put them on, and occupied himself with a pocket-book, and seemed to be totting up some figures.

"You guessed, of course, that I must have

something to say on that subject?" he said, raising his eyes from the page.

"I thought it possible," she answered, with an effort.

"I could not in the drawing-room, you know——"

"No, of course," she said, hastily, and the colour returned with two hot flushes to her cheeks.

There was in her bearing to this elderly gentleman an odd embarrassment, something of pain and shame; a wounded pride struggling through it.

She rose, and they walked together to the window.

"He has got his leave. His troop is still at Chatham. The doctor says he must go to some quiet country nook. He has been thinking of Beaumaris," said the old gentleman.

"Is he as beautiful as ever?" she asked. "Oh, why should I ask? What does it matter? Is there any gift that God gives his creatures that is not more or less a curse?"

"You should not talk in that wild way, Barbara. If people can't control their feelings, they can, at least, control their words. It is only an effort at first. It easily becomes a matter of habit. You shan't talk so to me."

She looked at him angrily for a moment of silence.

"You treat me with a contempt, sir, that you

never could have felt if I had not trusted you so madly," she cried, passionately.

The tone, fierce and plaintive, was lost on the phlegmatic old man in the black wig.

He delivered a little lecture, with his thin brown finger raised, and his exhortation was dry, but stern.

"You have been rash and self-willed; you have been to blame. Your unjust imputation shan't prevent my saying that, and whatever else truth requires. Your difficulty is the creation of your own passions. I don't say look your difficulty in the face, for it will look you in the face; but take the lesson it teaches, and learn self-control."

"Don't blame me for this. I met him first in a railway carriage, nearly two years ago. Who can prevent such accidental acquaintances? He was so attentive, and so agreeable, and so gentleman-like. I had chosen to travel alone, without even a maid. You'll say I had no business doing so. I say, at my years, there was nothing against it; it was more than four hours; there were other people in the carriage. I never meant to seek him out afterwards; it was the merest accident my learning even his name. When I met him next, it was in town, at Lady Stukely's. I recognised him instantly, but he did not know me, for my veil had been down all the time." This narra-

tive Lady Vernon was pouring out with the rapid
volubility of excitement. "I was introduced to
him there. Perhaps I have been a fool; but there
is no good, now, in telling me so. I have seen
him since, more than once, and gone where I
thought I was likely to see him, and I succeeded.
If I have been a fool, God knows I suffer. My
difficulty, you call it! My difficulty! My agony
is the right word. To love as I love, without
being loved, without being loved ever so little!"

"So much the better," said Mr. Dawe, phleg-
matically. "What are you driving at? You
ought to consider consequences. Don't you know
the annoyance, and possibly insane litigation, to
which your folly would lead? In a woman of
your years, Barbara, this sort of thing is inexcusable."

"Why did you come at all? Why did you
come in so suddenly, and—before people? Would
not a letter have answered? Hast thou found
me, oh! mine enemy?" she suddenly almost cried,
and clasped her fingers for a moment wildly upon
his arm.

"A letter?" he repeated.

"Yes, a letter. You should think. It would
have been more merciful," she answered, vehemently.

"Not when I had so many things to talk to you about," he retorted, quietly.

"I would have met you anywhere. You ought not to have come into the room so suddenly," she persisted. "You alone know my sad secret. You might have remembered that people are sometimes startled. You say I have no self-command. I think I have immense self-command. I think I am a stoic. I know how you tasked it, too. I knew you had something important to tell me, and that *he* was probably involved."

"H'm! Yes; I'm an old friend of yours, and I wish you well. And I'm Captain Vivian's friend, and was once his guardian, and I wish him well. And this kind of thing I don't approve of. And you'll get yourself spoken about; you *are* talked of. People saw you alone at Chatham last year; and if they come to connect your movements with his. think what it will be."

"He's the only person on earth I love, or ever shall love."

"Barbara, you forget your child, Maud Vernon," said the old man, with hard emphasis.

"I don't forget her," she answered, fiercely.

The old man turned away his head. There was no change of countenance: that, I believe, never changed; but the movement indicated disgust.

"I say I love him, with all my love, with *all*," she repeated.

"Be it so. Still, common prudence will suggest your keeping that love locked up in your own heart, a dead secret."

"I am determined, somehow or other, to meet him, and talk to him, and know him well," she persisted; "and you shall assist me."

"I'm wholly opposed to it."

"You'd not have me see him again?"

"No."

"Why? What are you? Who are you? Have you human sympathy? Good Heavens! Am I a free woman?" she broke out again, wildly.

"Certainly, quite free," said Mr. Dawe, cutting her short with a little tap on his snuff-box. "You can do it, Barbara, when you please; however, whenever, wherever you like best; only you have a right to my judgment, and I'm quite against it."

"I know, Mr. Dawe, you are my friend," she said, after a brief pause. "I know how I can trust you. I am impetuous, perhaps. I dare say you are right. You certainly would speak wisely if your counsels were addressed to some colder and happier woman. Why is it that to be cold, and selfish, and timid, is the only way to be happy on

earth? If I am sanguine, audacious, what you
will, I can't help it. You cannot understand me
— God knows all; for me to live any longer as I
am is worse than death. I'll endure it no longer.
Oh! if I could open my lips and tell him all!"

"There, that's it, you see! You are ready to
die now to be on more intimate terms with him;
and if you were you would be ready to die again,
as you say, to open your heart to him. Don't you
see? Don't you perceive what it is tending to?
Are you prepared for all that? If not, why
approach it? You would be in perpetual danger
of saying more than you think you should."

Mr. Dawe had probably not spoken quite so long
a sentence for more than a month.

"I may be a better listener, Mr. Dawe, in a
little time. Let us sit down. I want to ask you
about it. Tell me everything. What was his
illness?"

"Fever."

"Fever! and he was in great danger. Oh! my
darling, my darling, for how long?"

"For two days in great danger."

Her hands were clasped as she looked in his face,
and she went on.

"And there is no danger now? It is quite
over?"

" Quite," he repeated.

She looked up, her fingers raised a little, and a long shuddering sigh, like a sob, relieved her.

"I had the best advice—the two best men I could get from London. He's all right now; he's fairly under way, and nothing can go wrong; with common prudence, of course. I have the account here." He held his pocket-book by the corner, and shook it a little.

"He was near dying," she repeated. "Why didn't you tell me? I knew nothing of his danger."

"The doctors did not tell me the extent of it till it was over," he replied.

"Think what it would have been if he had died! I should have been in a madhouse. I should have killed myself."

"Don't, don't, don't. Nonsense. Come, you must not talk so. I admit it is a painful situation; but who has made it? You. Remember that, and control your—your vehemence."

"Has he been out? Is he recovering strength?"

"Yes. He has been out, and he has made way; but he is still an invalid."

"I want to know; I must know. Is there any danger still apprehended?"

"None; I give you my word," said Mr. Dawe, dryly.

" He is still very weak ?" she urged.

" Still weak, but gaining strength daily."

" How soon do the doctors think he will be quite himself ?"

" In five or six weeks."

" And his leave of absence, for how long is that ?"

" It has been extended ; about four weeks still to run."

" I think I know everything now ?" she said, slowly.

Mr. Dawe nodded acquiescence.

" He's not rich, Mr. Dawe ; and all this must cost a good deal of money. It is only through you I can be of any use."

" Yes ; I was his guardian, and am his trustee. I had a regard for his father, and his grandfather was essentially kind to me. But I have learned to regret that I ever undertook to interest myself specially in his affairs ; and you, Barbara, are the cause of that regret."

" You mustn't reproach me ; you know what I am," she pleaded.

Mr. Dawe responded with his usual inarticulate " H'm !" and an oracular nod.

" I can't help it ; I can't. Why are you so cruelly unreasonable ? Do you think I can learn a new character, and unlearn the nature that God gave me, in a moment ?"

"I say this. If you cultivate Captain Vivian's acquaintance further, it is against my opinion and protest. I don't expect either to have much weight. I think you incorrigible."

Lady Vernon coloured, and her eyes flashed. But she would not, and could not, quarrel with Mr. Dawe.

"Surely you can't pretend there is anything wrong in it?" she said, fiercely.

"I did not say there was. Extreme imprudence; reckless imprudence."

"You always said everything I did was reckless and imprudent."

"Not everything. Some things extremely. And what you propose, considering that you are no longer young, and know what the world is, appears to me a positively inexcusable folly."

"It is possible to prescribe limits and impose conditions upon oneself," she said, with an effort; "and if so, there need be no rashness in the matter, not the slightest."

"Possible? We know it's *not* possible with some people."

"You always hated me, sir."

"Tut, tut!"

"You never liked me."

"Pooh, pooh!"

" You have always thought ill of me."

" I have always wished you well, Barbara, and accident, I think, enabled me to understand you better than others. You have great faults, immense faults."

" All faults and no virtues, of course," she said, with a bitter little laugh.

" You are capable of strong and enduring attachments."

" Even that is something," she said, with an agitated smile, and burst into tears.

" This is very painful, Barbara," said the little man in the black wig, while a shadow of positive displeasure darkened his furrowed face. " I believe my first impression was right, and yours too. I begin to think I had no business coming to Roydon."

Lady Vernon got up, and walked toward the window, and then turned, and walked to the further end of the room, standing before a picture.

He could see that her handkerchief was busy drying her eyes.

With a womanly weakness she walked to the mirror close by, and looked into it, and perhaps was satisfied that the traces of this agitation were not very striking.

She returned to her place.

"I have been a fool. My saying so will perhaps save you trouble. I want to put you in funds again."

"When you please," said the old man. "Any time will answer. I have the figures here." His pocket-book was still in his hand. "But he has money enough of his own. He must think me a fool, paying all these expenses for him. And I think, Barbara, your doing so is a mischievous infatuation."

"And you would deny me this one pleasure!" she said.

"Enough, enough," he answers. "It was not about that I came here; that we could have settled by a letter. But I knew you would have fifty questions to ask. He has made up his mind to try change of air. I'm ignorant in such matters, and he has not made up his mind where to go."

"I have quite made up my mind upon that point," she answered.

"Well; and where?"

"Here," said Lady Vernon, once more in her cold, quiet way. "I'll ask him here."

"H'm!" said Mr. Dawe.

"Here," she repeated, with her old calm peremptoriness. "Here, at Roydon Hall. I'll receive him here, and he can't be quieter or better anywhere else, and you shall come with him."

It was now Mr. Dawe's turn to get up, which he did with a kind of jerk, and, checking some impulse, walked slowly round his chair, looking down on the carpet, and with a pretty wide circuit he came behind it, and resting his hands on its high back, and leaning over, he said, with a little pause, and a wag of his head to each word:

"Is there the least use in my arguing the point?"

"None."

"H'm!"

Mr. Dawe looked to the far corner of the room, with eyes askance, ruminating, and took a pinch of snuff, some of which shed a brown snow upon the cut pattern of the Utrecht velvet on the back of the chair.

"I can't say it is anything to me; nothing. I should be officious were I to say more to dissuade you from it. Only remember, I have no share in the responsibility of this, excuse me, most strange step. As I suppose he will be brought here, one way or other, in any case, I think I had better come with him, and stay a day or two. It will excite less observation, so——"

"Thank you so very much, Mr. Dawe," said

Lady Vernon, extending her hand, with an odd, eager gratitude in tone and countenance. "That is like yourself."

Mr. Dawe's usual "H'm!" responded to this little effusion, and with an ominous countenance he took her proferred hand in his dry grasp, and let it go almost in a moment.

Looking down on the carpet, he walked to the window, with his hands behind his back, and as, with furrowed jaws and pursed mouth, and a roll of his prominent eyes, he stood close to the pane of glass, down which the rain was no longer streaming, Lady Vernon opened her desk, and wrote a cheque for two hundred pounds, and coming to his side, she said :

"He does not suspect that he has a friend concealed?"

"Certainly not—certainly not," said Mr. Dawe, sharply.

"Will you apply this for me, and we can account another time? And you think me very ungrateful, Mr. Dawe, but indeed I am not. I only wish an opportunity may occur, if you could only point out some way. But you are so rich, and so happy. Well, some day, notwithstanding, I may be able to show you how I thank you. Let us return to the drawing-room."

As she passed the mirror, the lady glanced at her face again, and was satisfied.

"Yes," said Mr. Dawe, recurring to the matter of business, "I'll do that, and with respect to coming here, I say no more. Under protest, mind, I do it. Only let me have a line to say when you can receive us."

CHAPTER XXVII.

THE NUN'S WELL.

MAUD was found by her elders, on their return, nestled in a low chair, in one of those lazy moods in which one not only does nothing, but thinks nothing.

They were talking as they entered, and Maud turned her eyes merely in their direction, being far enough away to feel herself very little observed.

"You will surely stay to-night, Mr. Dawe?" said Lady Vernon.

"No, certainly; thank you very much. I have made up my mind," replied Mr. Dawe, dryly.

Miss Maud was observing this little man in the

wig with increased interest. There was in his manner, looks, and voice something of the familiarity of an old friend, she thought, without much of the liking.

Whatever the business which they discussed in the library, her mamma, she thought, was perfectly unruffled; but there were traces of displeasure in the old gentleman's demeanour.

"I ought to have told you that my cousin, Maximilla Medwyn, is staying here."

"She has returned, mamma; she will be down in a few minutes," said Maud.

"Oh! and we shall certainly have her here for some days. Will that tempt you to stay?"

"I like her well—very well, but I shall be off, notwithstanding," said the old gentleman, with a rigid countenance.

The sound of the gong announced luncheon.

"We are a very small party," she said, smiling. "I'm glad you're here to luncheon, at all events."

"I've had a biscuit and a glass of sherry."

"But that is not luncheon, you know," said Lady Vernon.

Maud wondered more and more why her mamma should take such unusual pains to conciliate this odd, grim old man. For her part, she did not know what to make of him. Ungainly, preposterous, obsolete as he was, she yet could not

assign him a place outside the line that encircles
gentlemen. There was not a trace of vulgarity in
the reserved and saturnine inflexibility of his face.
There was something that commanded her respect,
in the obvious contrast it presented to the vulgar
simper and sycophancy of the people who generally
sought "audiences" of her mother.

And Maud fancied when he looked at her,
that there was something of kindly interest dimly
visible through his dark and solemn lineaments.

"Luncheon and dinner," he said, "are with me
incompatible; and I prefer my dinner. My train,
I think, is due at six-twenty P.M. I suppose your
servant can find a Bradshaw, and I'll consult it
while you are at luncheon. Go, Barbara. Go,
pray; you make me uncomfortable."

The little old man sat himself down in an arm-
chair, took out his pocket-book, and seemed to
forget everything but the figures over which he
began to pore.

Miss Max joined the ladies at luncheon.

"Well, we shall find him in the drawing-room,"
she said, reconciling herself to her disappointment. "It is a long time since I saw him. But
I dare say he's not much changed. Wigs wear
wonderfully."

"So do ugly men," added Lady Vernon, carelessly.

So luncheon proceeded. And when it was over, the three ladies came to the drawing-room, and, looking round, discovered that Mr. Dawe was gone.

A minute after, Maud saw him walking under the trees of the avenue, with his broad-leafed, low-crowned hat on, and a slow, stiff tread, and his silk umbrella in his hand doing the office of a walking-stick. It was pleasant sunshine now.

The blue sky was clear and brilliant, and only a few white clouds near the horizon accounted for the rain-drops that still glittered on the blades of grass. Stepping carefully in the centre of the path, little Mr. Dawe, now and then shouldering his umbrella. and turning and looking about him, like a man reviving old recollections and scanning alterations, disappeared slowly from view, over the stile, leaving Miss Maud very curious.

" I'll put on my things, and try to find him," said Miss Max, in a fuss, and was speedily seen emerging from the hall-door in pursuit.

His walk being slow and meditative, his active pursuer did succeed in overtaking him. She knew very well that he was glad to see her, though his rigid features gave no sign, and he shook hands very kindly.

When these greetings were over, he answered her question by saying briefly :

"No, I shan't dine.   I'm off."

"Without bidding Barbara good-bye!" exclaimed Miss Medwyn, drawing herself up in
amazement.

"I've left my farewell in the hall.   The footman will find it."

"A note, I suppose?"

"H'm," acquiesced the little gentleman.   "My
carriage will take me up in the village;" and he
nodded gravely to the distant tower of Roydon
Church, which happily did not return that salutation, though he continued to stare solemnly at it
for some seconds, and ended by a second slighter
nod.

"That is not a pretty compliment to me," she
said.   "I think you might have stayed till to-
morrow."

He nodded only, and silence followed.

"Well, I see you won't."

Another pause, and a more impatient "H'm,"
and a quick shake of the head.

"So as that can't be," she resumed, "and as all
things are so uncertain in this life, that we may
possibly never meet again, I'll walk a little way
with you towards the village."

Mr. Dawe nodded his usual sign of acquiescence.

"And now you must tell me," she said, as they
walked at a leisurely pace along the path which

winds gently among the old timber, "what on earth brought you here? Has anything wonderful happened; is anything wonderful going to happen?"

"A word or two with Barbara," he said.

"You don't mean to tell me it is a secret?" said she.

"If it be, it is none of mine," he replied.

"Well but you can tell me generally, what it is about," she insisted.

"H'm! Ask Barbara," he answered.

"You mean, it is a secret, and you won't tell it?" she said.

Mr. Dawe left this inference unanswered.

"You found Barbara very little altered?" said Miss Max.

"As self-willed and unwise as ever," he replied.

"Ho! Then she wants to do something foolish?"

"She can do that when she pleases," he remarked. "Do you know the Tinterns, who live near?"

"Yes, pretty well," she answered, rather curious to know why he should ask.

"What do you think of them?"

"I rather dislike Mr. Tintern, I neither like nor dislike his wife, and I like his daughter very much indeed. His son I don't know: he is with his regiment in India," she answered. "Why do you ask?"

"You are as inquisitive as ever, Maximilla," he said.

"I've just satisfied your curiosity about the Tinterns, and you can't complain fairly of my question. I think your business with Barbara had something to do with them."

"You are sagacious," he observed; but whether he spoke in good faith or in irony his countenance helped her nothing to discover.

"Come, you must tell me. Are the Tinterns involved in the foolish thing she is going to do?" the lady insisted.

"She is going to do a foolish thing, and you, probably, will never know what makes it so particularly foolish; that is, unless she carries out her folly to its climax."

"I may possibly guess more than you suppose," Miss Medwyn said.

But this remark led to nothing.

"You don't know young Tintern, you say, but you like his sister. Why?" asked Mr. Dawe.

"I like her because she is really nice—one of the very nicest girls I ever knew."

"Ha! Then, I hope she doesn't depend altogether on her father, for they say he has lost money?" said Mr. Dawe.

"She is not well provided for, although her mother was an heiress, you know; but there is something trifling settled on her."

"Well for her she doesn't depend altogether on Tintern. I'm told he is a distressed man, or likely soon to be so," he said.

"But, to come back to Barbara," resumed Maximilla: "I think you ought to exercise your influence to prevent her from taking any foolish step, particularly one which may affect others."

"I have none."

"If you haven't, who has?"

"No one ever had, for her good."

"For my part, I never knew what to think of her," said Miss Medwyn.

"I did," said Mr. Dawe.

He stopped short, and looked straight at her, being about her own height, which, even for a woman, was nothing very remarkable. His dark face looked darker, and his prominent brown eyes were inflexibly fixed on her, as he spoke a rather longer harangue than usual.

"She is a great dissembler." said Mr. Dawe. "She is proud. She has the appearance of coldness, and she is secretly passionate and violent. She is vindictive. All that is concealed. She has a strong will. People know that; but it is not inflexibility founded on fixed data. It is simply irresistible impulse. There is nothing fixed in her but a few likings and hatreds. Principles in the high sense, that is, involving the submission of a life to maxims of duty, she has none; and she thinks herself a paragon."

Maximilla laughed, and they resumed their walk, when Mr. Dawe had ended his speech.

"That seems rather a severe delineation, Mr. Dawe," said Maximilla Medwyn, with another little laugh and a shrug.

"It is true. I would repeat it to herself, if it could do her any good."

They followed the path, Miss Medwyn chatting, after her manner, gaily, until they nearly reached the stile at the village road.

"So here we part, Mr. Dawe."

Mr. Dawe gave her one of his oracular looks, and took her hand in his hard fingers.

"And it is very ill-natured of you not telling me what I asked you," she called after him.

Bestriding the stile, he looked back with the same solemnity, raised his broad-leafed hat, and disappeared on the other side, and Maximilla could not help laughing a little at the awful gravity and silence of the apparition which went down behind the wall.

The day was now brilliant, and Miss Medwyn

was tempted to walk home by a path still prettier, though a little circuitous.

It was a favourite walk of hers long ago. Perhaps it was the visit of Mr. Dawe, with whom in old times she had often walked these out-of-the-way paths, that suggested this little ramble.

The lofty trees close about the path that she had now chosen, and gradually beset and overhang it in the densest shadow. Walking in the open air, on a sunny day, you could not fancy so deep a darkness anywhere. This is, of course, in the leafy days, when the tall elms, whose boughs cross and mix above, are laden with their thick dark foliage.

The darkness and silence of this narrow path are here so curiously deep, that it is worth going a mile or two out of one's way to visit it; and fancy will play a nervous wayfarer as many tricks in this strange solitude as in a lonely night walk.

At the side of this path, nearly in its darkest part, is a well, under an arch. It is more properly a spring, rising at this point, and overflowing its stone basin, and escapes, in a gush, through a groove cut in the flag that encloses it, in front. Two iron cups, hanging by chains, invite the passenger to drink of the icy water that with ceaseless plash and gurgle descends from the opening.

With a slow step on the light mossy turf she draws near this remembered point of interest. Her eyes have grown accustomed to the clear shadow. Two steps lead down to the level at which one can take the iron cup, and drink from this cold well.

If outside all is shadowy, you may suppose how obscure it is within this low arch.

As she looks, she sees something rise within it. It is the figure of a man, who has just been stooping for a draught from the spring. His back is turned toward her.

We do not know how habitually we rely upon the protection of the upright among our fellow-men, until accident isolates us, and we confront a possible villain in a lonely place. There was no reason to suspect this man above other strangers. But a sense of her helplessness frightened her.

She stepped back, as most old ladies, with presence of mind, would have done under the circumstances. And very still, from her place of comparative concealment, she sees this faint shadow emerge, in shade less deep, and she discerns the long neck, lank jaws, and white eyeball of Elihu Lizard.

The lady pursed her mouth and frowned, as she might at a paragraph in the newspaper describing a horror; and she drew a little further back, and as much behind the huge trunk of the tree at the edge of the path as she could with the power of still peeping at Mr. Lizard.

That lank wayfarer, in such a place, having, we must suppose, a quieter conscience than Miss Max, did not trouble himself to grope and peep about for spies, or other waylayers, among the trees, and having wiped his mouth on his sleeve, he sopped his lank face all over with his coloured handkerchief, which he rolled into a ball, and pitched into his hat. Next he replaced his hat on his head, and gave it a little adjusting jerk.

Then Mr. Lizard threw his head back, so as to look up to the groining of branches above him. She could not tell exactly, so dark it was, what expression his odious countenance wore. Her active fancy saw a frown one moment, a smile the next, and then a grimace. Though these uncertain distortions seemed to flicker over it, I dare say his lean face was quiet enough then, and having popped something, which I conjecture to have been a plug of tobacco, into his mouth, he shouldered his stick with a little preliminary flourish, and set out again upon his march in the direction from whence she had just come.

This apparition gave a new direction to her thoughts. She waited quietly till she could hear his steps no more. She wondered whether he had

been up to the Hall; but she recollected that this
particular path crossed the park; there was a right
of way by it, and therefore he need not have
diverged to the house, nor have asked any one's
leave to cross the grounds by it.

There remained the question, why was he here?
Were she and Maud never to get rid of that odious
attendant? She quickened her step homeward,
and was glad when she emerged into the open light.

CHAPTER XXVIII.

INQUIRY.

Turning into another walk, at her left, she approached the house, and saw Maud looking about her, as she stood in the midst of the scarlet and blue verbenas in the Dutch garden at the side of the Hall.

She signed to the old lady, smiling, as she emerged.

"I have been looking all round for you, and almost repenting I had not gone with you. I really began to think he had run away with you."

"Walked away, you mean; he does everything deliberately. He never ran in his life," replies the old lady.

"Well—well—and ——" The young lady stole

a quick glance over her shoulder to be sure
they were not observed, and lowering her voice
very much as they got nearer, she continued
eagerly, " and tell me what he said. Did he tell
you anything?"

" Well, he thinks he told me nothing, and intended to tell me nothing, but he did tell me a
great deal," answered Miss Max, smiling shrewdly,
" and I don't know whether you will be glad or
sorry, but the upshot is, putting everything together, I am nearly certain that your mamma
intends marrying, and that he is strongly against
it."

" Really!" exclaimed Maud, stopping short, for
they were walking very slowly, side by side.

" He did not say so in so many words, mind, but
I can't account for what he said on any other sup-
position," said Miss Max. " Has not she been
very diplomatic? I don't know that any living
creature but I suspected what those mysterious
excursions could be about. You see Mr. Coke
jumped to the same conclusion when I told him
the facts. I can't understand that kind of thing.
What can be the pleasure of going through life,
without a human being to whom you ever tell anything you either feel or intend? But she was
always the same. She never trusted any one, as
long as I remember her."

Maud listened to all this very thoughtfully.

"Tell me, like a darling, what you collect it from; tell me everything he said," after a considerable silence, Maud asked.

So Maximilla Medwyn repeated her conversation with Mr. Dawe with praiseworthy minuteness.

"What do you think of it?" she asked, in conclusion.

"I think it looks extremely like what you say," Maud replied, looking down thoughtfully.

"And do you like it?"

"I can't say I do. It is not a thing I have much thought about—mamma's marrying; but if she wishes——"

She stopped suddenly, and Maximilla saw, to her surprise, that she was crying.

"Pooh, pooh! my dear child, take care," said Miss Max. "Goodness knows who may see you. I had not an idea you cared so much. When I talked to you before about it you didn't seem to mind."

"I don't know; it didn't seem so likely or so near," she said, making an effort, and drying her eyes hastily. "And really I don't know, as you say, whether I ought to be glad or sorry."

"Well, for the present, we'll put that particular inquiry aside, for I want to tell you that horrid one-eyed man has pursued us, and I saw him at the old well, in the dark walk, just now. We must make out whether he was at the house. I dare say Jones can find out all about him."

Full of this idea they returned together to the house; but no such person, so far as they could make out, had been there.

Jones, again charged to inquire, failed to discover anything.

"You see he has no business, or even pretence of business, at the house," said Miss Max. "I think he's watching you. It can be for no good purpose; and if I were you, I should tell your mamma."

"Why mamma? I mean, why should I tell any one?" She looked uncomfortably at Miss Medwyn.

"I think your mamma ought to know it, and I think it is better that people should know that you observe it."

Their eyes met for a moment, and were again averted.

"Yes, I think I will go to mamma, and tell her," said the young lady. "Shall I find you here when I come back?"

They were in the hall at the time.

"Yes, I'll wait here," she answered.

Lady Vernon was alone in the library. Maud knocked at the door, and her mother's voice told her to come in.

She did so, and found Lady Vernon writing. She raised her eyes only for a moment, and said, with a cold glance at her daughter:

"Have you anything to say, Maud?"

"Only this. I wish to tell you, mamma, that a very ill-looking, elderly man, who has been following my Cousin Max and me from place to place, during the whole of our little excursion, evidently tracking and watching us, for what purpose we can't guess, has turned up, to-day, in the grounds. Maximilla saw him at the Nun's Well, in the dark walk, to-day. He is blind of one eye, and pretends to be travelling for a religious society, and his name is Elihu Lizard."

She paused.

Lady Vernon had resumed her writing, and said, with her eyes on the line her pen was tracing:

"Well?"

"I only wanted to ask, mamma, whether you knew anything of any such person?" said Maud.

"A man blind of one eye, what was he doing?" said Lady Vernon, dropping each word slowly, as she continued her writing.

"Following us from place to place, everywhere we went, and we really grew at last quite frightened and miserable," said the young lady.

"I think, Maud, you should endeavour to be less governed by your imagination. There is no one admitted to Roydon who is not a proper person, and, in all respects, unexceptionable. You must know that," said Lady Vernon, looking in her face with a cold stare, "and I don't think, within the precincts of Roydon, that you or Max have anything to fear from the machinations of blind elderly men, and I really have no time to discuss such things just now." And Lady Vernon, with imperious displeasure, turned and wrote her letter diligently.

So Maud turned and left the stately seclusion of that apartment, and returned through the other rooms to the hall, where she found Miss Max.

"I don't think she knows anything about him," said Maud.

"If she does not, that only makes it more unpleasant," answered the old lady.

And they went out again together for a walk.

The interrogation of Lady Vernon had not resulted, I think, in anything very satisfactory. Maud, however, did not venture to renew it; and in their after rambles in the grounds or the village of Roydon, neither she nor Miss Max encountered any more the ill-favoured apparition of Elihu Lizard.

The monotonous life of Roydon went drowsily on.

At the entreaty of Maud, Miss Medwyn prolonged her stay, which she interrupted only by a visit of a day or half a day, now and then, to a neighbouring house ; and so a week or more had flown, when an incident occurred which, in the end, altered, very seriously, the relations of many people in and about Roydon Hall.

CHAPTER XXIX.

CAPTAIN VIVIAN.

ONE evening, Maximilla Medwyn and Maud returned from a drive, just in time to dress for dinner. The sun was setting as they descended from the open carriage and mounted the steps.

Compared with the flaming sky and ruddy sunlight outside, deep was the shadow of the hall as they entered. But Miss Max discerned in that shade the figure of a little man standing in the background.

She stopped for a moment, exclaiming:

"Good gracious! Is this you, Mr. Dawe?"

"How do you do, Miss Medwyn?" replied the small figure, advancing into the reflected glow that entered through the hall-door, and revealing the veritable black wig and mahogany face of that saturnine humorist.

"I hope you are not going already?" said she. "We have not been out two hours, have we, Maud?"

Thus brought into prominence, Maud greeted the old gentleman, who then made answer to Miss Medwyn.

"I stay till to-morrow or next day."

"Well, that's an improvement on your last visit, short as it is," she replied. "Do you know, I had quite made up my mind that we were never to meet in this world again."

"So much for prescience. We are not witches, Maximilla," observed the little gentleman, dryly.

"Though we should not look the part badly, you and I," she rejoined, with a laugh; "one thing I do predict: you'll meet Mr. Tintern at dinner to-day; you were asking about him, you remember."

"H'm!" he responded, with a roll of his eyes.

And with this brief greeting the ladies went up to their rooms, and Mr. Dawe, more slowly, followed to his.

When Miss Maud returned to the drawing-room, Mr. Tintern, having been at the Wymering Sessions to meet his brother magistrates, had not yet arrived. Lady Vernon had not returned, but a stranger was there.

There was no one in the room, except a young man, rather tall and slight. He had brown hair and light moustache, and was, if not actually handsome, certainly good-looking, and nothing could be more quiet and gentleman-like than his air and dress.

He had the pallor and general languor of an invalid. He appeared about thirty; but he had been ill, and was possibly younger. He was leaning on the chimney-piece, and, I think, was actually looking at himself in the great mirror over it, as Maud came into the room.

It was a little awkward, perhaps, there being no one to introduce him; but, notwithstanding, in a little while they were very cheerfully engaged in conversation, though not exactly of importance or novelty enough to very deeply interest my readers.

They had not been so employed very long, when Lady Vernon appeared.

"Captain Vivian, I must introduce you to my daughter."

Captain Vivian bowed.

"You have never been in this part of the world before?" said Lady Vernon. "I think you said so?"

"No. Coventry, I think, is about the nearest point of any interest I'm acquainted with."

"Oh! That is quite a journey; but there is a good deal worth seeing near us; we can plan all that to-morrow. I only hope our fine weather may continue," said Lady Vernon. "Oh, Mr. Dawe! you came in so quietly, I did not see you. I dare say you knew your old room again. You used to like it long ago, so I thought I'd put you into it."

"Thanks. Yes—h'm!" said Mr. Dawe, solemnly, with a mysterious ogle, as if it was a good room to conjure in. "I remember it."

Captain Vivian was talking to Miss Vernon.

"How pale he looks!" Lady Vernon almost whispered to Mr. Dawe, her eyes covertly following the young man's movements. "He is fatigued— he is doing too much. Make him sit down."

Mr. Dawe nodded. He approached the young man and said a few words to him.

"Thank you very much, Mr. Dawe; but I really am not the least fatigued. I have not felt so strong I don't know when."

"Yes; but you *are* fatigued, and you must sit down," said Mr. Dawe, raising his brown hand and laying it on the young man's shoulder with an imperious pressure.

But before he had accomplished his purpose,

Mr. Tintern, who had arrived, claimed his attention by playfully taking his disengaged hand, and saying:

"You won't look at me, Mr. Dawe. You are not going to cut your old friend, I hope?"

Mr. Dawe looked round. Tall Mr. Tintern stood before him, with a sort of wintry sunshine in his smile, which was not warm; his false teeth and light eyes were shining coldly on him.

Since they last met, Mr. Tintern's hair has grown almost white, but, as it was always light, this does not alter the character of his countenance, which, however, has grown puffy and wrinkled, with an infinity of fine lines, that indicate nothing bolder or higher, perhaps, than cunning.

Mr. Tintern is one of those pleasant fellows who is always glad to see everybody, and whose hand is always open to shake that of his neighbour; who can smile on people he does not like, as easily as he laughs at jokes he does not understand. For the rest, he parts with his condolences more easily than with his shillings, and taking on himself the entire burden of sympathy, he leaves to others the coarser enjoyment of relieving suffering by sacrifices of money or trouble.

"I never cut my friends," says Mr. Dawe. "I

don't think I have five in the world. That is a luxury for people who have money."

"You have some very good ones, out of the five, in this part of the world, at all events, and I only hope you remember them as well as they remember you," replies Mr. Tintern, with a playful effervescence.

Mr. Dawe makes one of his stiff bows; but they shake hands, and Mr. Tintern holds the hard brown fingers of his "friend" longer in his puffy white hand than Mr. Dawe seems to care for.

"Time flies, Mr. Dawe," says Mr. Tintern, with a little plaintive smile and a shake of the head.

"Yes, sir; and we alter very much," answers Mr. Dawe.

"Not all—not all," says Mr. Tintern, who does not acquiesce in the approaches of senility: "at least I can vouch for you."

And he lays his soft hand caressingly on Mr. Dawe's arm.

"H'm!" says Mr. Dawe.

And the interval that follows hears from him no return of the little flattery.

"We have been considering a good many things to-day after our session; putting our heads together. It will interest Lady Vernon," says Mr. Tintern, cheerfully. "By-the-bye, Lady Vernon, a question is to be submitted to you for your decision, and we so hope you will say 'Yes.' We are thinking, if you approve, of moving for a presentment next assizes, for a short road, only three and a half miles, connecting the two roads from the northern end of Wymering, across by Linton Grange, to meet the Trafford road, about a quarter of a mile at this side of Stanbridge. But it is nearly all Roydon property, I need not tell you, and of course all depends upon you, and we were consulting as to how best to submit it, so as to obtain your sanction and assistance."

"I think something ought to be done," says Lady Vernon. "I said so before, and I shall be very happy to talk with my steward about it, and the surveyor can call here; but I'm not so sure that those are the best points. I shall look at the map to-morrow. I traced the line; I'm nearly certain I did what I thought best. You shall hear from me in time for the assizes."

Miss Max had entered, and Mr. Dawe, in his grim, ungainly way, presented Captain Vivian. You might see that the old lady looked a little inquisitively at him, of course very cautiously, and that something was passing in her mind.

There was not much time, indeed, for speculation, and hardly any for a little talk with this young gentleman, for the whole party in a few minutes went away to the dining-room, where they were all presently much more agreeably employed.

Nothing very worthy of record occurred during dinner, nor after that meal, until the gentlemen had followed the ladies to the drawing-room, and then a little psychological discussion arose over the tea-table.

"I have been reading a novel, Barbara," said Miss Max, "and the heroine is made to fall in love with the hero before he has made a sign, and, for anything she knows, he is quite indifferent. Now it strikes me that I don't remember a case of that kind, and I am collecting opinions. Maud says it is impossible. Mr. Dawe, on the contrary, thinks it quite on the cards. Captain Vivian agrees with Maud that the thing could not be, and now I want to know what you and Mr. Tintern can add for the enlightenment of an old maid in her perplexity?"

Now this question interrupted a dialogue very earnest, and spoken very low, between Lady Vernon and Mr. Tintern, who were sitting quite far enough apart from the others to make their conversation inaudible to the rest of the party. That dialogue had been carried on thus:

"You may suppose what it has been to me," Lady Vernon said, "the suspense and torture of mind, although, possibly, of course, it may never be."

"You have my warmest and deepest sympathy, Lady Vernon; I need not tell you," answered Mr. Tintern, closing his eyes, with a look of proper concern, and a plaintive shake of his head, "and I feel very much honoured, I assure you, by your selecting me for this, I may say, very deplorable confidence; and I shall, I need hardly add, consider it a very sacred trust. But you have, of course, mentioned it to other friends?"

"Only to one, of whose good sense I have a very high opinion indeed," said she.

"Mr. Dawe?" suggested Mr. Tintern.

"Certainly not," said Lady Vernon, with a quick glance towards that solemn little figure. "He is about the last person on earth I should speak to on the subject."

"Oh, I see," murmured Mr. Tintern, deferentially, throwing at the same moment a vast deal of caution into his countenance; "it is a kind of thing, of course, that requires immense circumspection."

"Yes," replied the lady, "and I intended——" It was at this word that Miss Max's inopportune inquiry broke in.

"I did not hear your question," says Lady Vernon, a little bored by the interruption.

Miss Max repeated it.

"Well, Mr. Tintern, what do you say?" she asked.

"Why, really," said Mr. Tintern, working hard to get up a neat reply, and smiling diligently, "where there is so much fascination of mind or of beauty, or of both, as we often see, in this part of the world, I can hardly fancy, eh?—the lady's being allowed time to be the first to fall in love—ha, ha, ha!—really—upon my honour—and that's my answer."

And he looked as if he thought it was not a bad answer.

"And now, Barbara, what do you say?" persisted Miss Max.

"I? I've no opinion upon it," said Lady Vernon, with a little laugh; but a close observer could have discovered anger in her eye. "I will think it over, and, in a day or two, I shall be able to aid you with my valuable opinion."

And she turned again to Mr. Tintern, who asked, glancing at Captain Vivian:

"Mr. Dawe, does he make any stay in the country?"

"I don't know. I shall be very happy to make him stay here as long as I can. Captain Vivian, that young man, is his friend, and, it seems, was his ward, and as he could not leave him—he has been ill, and requires looking after—Mr. Dawe asked me if he might bring him here, and so I make him welcome also."

"A very gentleman-like, nice young fellow he is," said Mr. Tintern.

And so that little talk ended.

Mr. Tintern went his way, and the little party broke up, and the bedroom candles glided along the galleries, and the guests had soon distributed themselves in their quarters.

But that night an odd little incident did occur.

Miss Max had, after her usual little talk with Maud, bid her good-night, and her busy head was now laid on her pillow. The glimmer of a night-light cheered her solitude, and she had just addressed herself seriously to sleep, when an un-expected knock at her door announced a visitor.

She thought it was her maid, and said:

"Do come in, and take whatever you want, and let me be quiet."

But it was not her maid, but Lady Vernon, who came in, with her candle in her hand, and closed the door.

"Ho! Barbara? Well, what is it?" she said, wondering what she could want.

"Are you quite awake?" asked Lady Vernon.

"Perfectly; that is, I was going to settle; but it doesn't matter."

"Well, I shan't detain you long," said Lady Vernon, placing the candle on the table. "I could not sleep without asking you what you meant, for I'm sure you had a meaning, by asking me the question you did to-night."

She spoke a little hurriedly, and her eyes looked extremely angry, but her tones were cold.

"The only question I asked was about first love," began Miss Max.

"Yes; and I ask you what did you mean, for you did mean something, by putting so very odd a question to me?" she replied.

"Mean? What did I mean?" said Miss Max, sitting up straight in a moment, so that her face was at least as well lighted as her visitor's. "I assure you I meant nothing on earth, and I don't know what you mean by putting such a question to me."

The handsome eyes of Lady Vernon were fixed on her doubtfully.

"You used to be frank, Maximilla. Why do you hesitate to speak what is in your mind?" said Lady Vernon, sharply.

"Used to be—I'm always frank. As I told you before, there was nothing in my mind; but I think there's something in yours."

"I only wanted to know if you intended any insinuation, however ridiculous. I fancied there was a significance in your manner, and as I could not comprehend it, I asked you to define, as one doesn't care to have surmises affecting oneself afloat in the mind of a friend, without at least learning what they are."

"I had no surmises of the kind; but you have certainly gone the very way to fill my head with them. What could you have fancied I meant?"

"Suppose I thought that you meant that I had made overtures of marriage to my husband before he had declared himself. That would have been untrue and offensive."

"Such an idea never entered my mind—never could have—because I knew all about it as well as you did. That's mere nonsense, my dear child."

"Well, then, there's nothing else you could mean, and so I'm glad I came. I believe it is always best to be a little out-spoken, at the risk of a few hot words, than to keep anything in reserve among friends, and you and I are very old friends, Max. Good-night. I have not disturbed you much?"

And she kissed her.

"Not a bit, dear. Good-night, Barbara."

And Lady Vernon disappeared as swiftly as she came, leaving a new problem for Maximilla's active mind to work on.

CHAPTER XXX.

A VISIT.

In the morning Lady Vernon was more than usually affectionate when she greeted Miss Max.

When the little party met in the small room that opens into the chapel, where, as we know, Mr. Penrhyn, the secretary, officiated at morning prayers, Lady Vernon actually drew her cousin Maximilla to her and kissed her.

"Making reparation I suppose," thought Maximilla. "But there was no occasion, I was not hurt."

And by the suggestion involved in this unusual demonstration, good Miss Max's fancy was started on a wild tour of entertaining conjecture respecting her reserved cousin, Barbara, and the possible bearing of that curious question upon the sensibilities of the handsome woman of three-and-forty, who had not yet contracted a single wrinkle or grey hair; and I am sorry to say that the measured intonation of Mr. Penrhyn, the secretary, as he duly read his chapter from the First Book of Chronicles, sounded in her ears faint and far away, as the distant cawing of the rooks.

This morning service was now over, and the little party gathered round the breakfast-table.

Seen in daylight, Captain Vivian looked ill and weak enough. He was not up to the walking, riding, and rough out-door amusements of a country house. That was plain. He must lounge in easy-chairs, or lie his length on a sofa, and be content, for the present, to traverse the country with his handsome but haggard eyes only.

Those eyes are blue, his hair light brown and silken, his moustache soft and golden. It is a Saxon face, and good-looking.

There is no dragoonery or swagger about this guest; he is simply a well-bred gentleman, and, in plain clothes, as completely divested of the conventional, soldierly manner, as if he had never stood before a drill-sergeant.

Whether it is a consequence of his illness, I can't say, but he looks a little sad.

In a house now and then so deserted and always

so quiet as Roydon, the sojourn of a guest so unexceptionable, and also so agreeable, would have
been at any time very welcome.

A little time ago, indeed, Maud might have
thought this interruption of their humdrum life
pleasanter. She had a good deal now to think of.

"What an inheritance of pictures you have,"
said Captain Vivian. There is a seat outside the
window, and on this the invalid was taking his
ease, while Miss Max and Maud Vernon, seated
listlessly within, talked with him through the open
window. "I think portraits are the most glorious
and interesting of all possessions; I mean, of
course, family portraits."

"If one could only tell whose portraits they
are," said Maud, with a little laugh. "I know
about twenty, I think, and, Max, you know nearly
forty, don't you? And I don't know who knows
the rest. There is a list somewhere; grandpapa
made it out, I believe. But they are not all even
in that."

"I look round on them with a vague awe." He
said: "Artists and sitters, so long dead and gone;
I wonder whether their ghosts come back to look
at their work again, or to see what they once were
like. I envy you all those portraits. Aren't you
proud of them, Miss Vernon?"

"I suppose I ought to be," replied Maud. "I

dare say I should be if they were treated with
a little more respect. But when one meets one's
ancestors peeping from behind doors, shouldering
one another for want of room in galleries and in
lobbies, hid away in corners or with their backs to
the wall half-way up the staircase, they lose something of their dignity, and it becomes a little hard
to be proud of them."

"Such long lines of ancestors running so far
back into perspective!" said the invalid, languidly.
" Think of those who look back without a single
lamp to light the past! I knew a man who was
well born, his parents both unquestionably of good
family, first his mother, then his father died, when
he was but two years old," Captain Vivian continued, looking down, as he talked, on the veining
of the oak seat, along which he was idly running
his pencil. " His fate was very odd. He found
himself with money bequeathed to him by his
father, and with a guardian who had hardly known
that father, but who. I dare say half from charity,
the father being on his death-bed, undertook the
office. Of course if my friend's father had lived
a little longer, the guardian would have learnt from
his own lips all particulars respecting his charge.
But his death came too swiftly. There was no
mystery intended, of course; the money was in
foreign stocks, and was collected and brought to

England as the will directed, and neither he nor his guardian know as much as they would wish of the family of either parent. So there he is, quite isolated; a good-natured fellow, I believe. It gives him something to think about; and I assure you it is perfectly true. I was thinking what that poor fellow would give for such a flood of light upon his ancestry as your portraits throw upon yours."

"Perhaps he has made it all out by this time," suggested Miss Max.

"I don't think he has," said Captain Vivian.

"And what is his name?" inquired the old lady.

"Well, I'm afraid I ought not to mention his name," he said, looking up. "It does not trouble him much now, I think, and I dare say it has caused him more pain than it is worth. Here comes a carriage," he said, raising his head. "Your avenue is longer than it appears. it is so wide. What magnificent trees!"

"Who are they, I wonder; the bishop or the dean?" said curious Miss Max.

"It may be the Manwarings. We called there a few days ago," said Maud.

"The liveries look like brown and gold, as well as I can see," said Captain Vivian, who had stood up and was looking down the avenue.

"Oh, it is the Tinterns, then," said Maud.

"Chocolate and gold, yes," assented Miss Max. "I hope so much that charming creature, Miss Tintern, is in the carriage. You'd be charmed with her, Captain Vivian."

"I dare say I should. But I am an awfully dull person at present, and I rather shrink from being presented. Mr. Tintern, from what I saw of him last night, appears to be a good-natured, agreeable man?"

This was thrown out rather in the tone of an inquiry; but Captain Vivian did not wait for an answer; and, instead, moved slowly towards the hall-door, and before the Tinterns' carriage had reached the low balustrade of those ponds on which the swans and water-lilies float, he was in the drawing-room.

"I'm ashamed to say, I'm a little bit tired," said he to Miss Max; and pale and languid he did, indeed, look. "And I think till this little visit is over I'll get into the next room, and look over some of those books of prints. You must not think me very lazy; but if you knew what I was a week ago, you'd think me a Hercules now."

So, slowly, Captain Vivian withdrew to the quieter drawing-room beyond this room, and sat him down before a book in the window, and turned over the pages, alone.

In the mean time, agreeable Mr. Tintern has

arrived, and his extremely pretty daughter has come with him.

She and Maud kiss, as young lady friends will, with more or less sincerity, after a long absence.

They make a very pretty contrast. the blonde and the dark beauty, Miss Tintern having golden hair and blue eyes, and Maud Vernon large dark grey eyes and brown hair.

So these young persons begin to talk together. while Lady Vernon and Mr. Tintern converse more gravely, a little way off, on themes that interest them more than flower-shows, fashions, and the coming ball at Wymering. Good Miss Max, who, in spite of her grave years, likes a little bit of frivolity, joins the young people, and has her laugh and gossip with them very cosily.

Having disposed of the Wymering ball, and talked over the statue of Mr. Howard in the church a little, and passed on to some county marriages likely to be, and said a word or two on guipure work, and the fashions, Miss Max said:

"I did not see your flowers at the Grange; I'm told they are perfectly lovely. The shower came on, you know; I was to have seen them."

"Oh, yes, it was so unlucky," says Miss Tintern. "Yes, I think they are very good. Don't you, Maud?"

" Yes, wonderful," answers Maud; " they throw us, I know, quite into shade.''

" I think you are great florists in this part of the world," says Miss Max.   " I thought I was very well myself; but I find I'm a mere nobody among you.   You have got, of course, that new Dutch hyacinth.   It is so beautiful, and so immense—white, and so waxen.   What is its name, Maud ?"

Maud gave the name of this beautiful monster.

" No; I'm sure we haven't got it," answers Ethel Tintern.   " I should have liked so to see it."

" We have one," says Maud, " the last, I think, still in its best looks ; they are very late.   I saw it in the next room.   Come and see."

In the histories of a thousand men, I suppose it has not happened six times, possibly in that of ten thousand, not half so often, that a young man should be surprised, in a deep sleep, over a book, by two young ladies so beautiful, and in whose eyes he wished, perhaps, to appear agreeable.

When the young ladies had pushed open the door, they stood for a moment beside it talking, and then, coming in, Maud Vernon pointed out the flower they had come to examine.

And, as they looked, admired, and talked, accidentally her eye lighted on the invalid, as he sat in the window, one hand on his book, his book slanting from his knee, and he with closed eyes and head sunk on his other hand, in a deep sleep. She exchanged a glance with her companion, and a faint smile and a nod.

The young ladies returned to the drawing-room; and when they had left the room a very few seconds, the slumbering invalid, without disturbing his attitude, looked after them curiously from the corner of his now half-opened eye, and listened. Then he turned his chair, so as better to avert his face, and, without stirring, continued to listen.

But they did not return. And as Mr. Tintern proposed lunching at Hartstonge Hall, he and his pretty daughter very soon took their leave, and Captain Vivian watched them quietly from the window, as they got into the open carriage and drove away.

" What a nice girl Ethel Tintern is. I like her so very much," said Miss Max.

" Yes," said Lady Vernon, " but I did not think her looking well, did you ?"

" Very pretty, but perhaps a little pale," acquiesced Miss Max.

" Very pale, indeed," says Lady Vernon; " when she was going I was quite struck with it. Did you ever see her before, Mr. Dawe ?"

" No," answered that gentleman promptly from

the recess of the window, where he was reading a note.

"I saw you look at her a good deal, Mr. Dawe," said Maximilla, "and I know you thought her very pretty."

"H'm!" said Mr. Dawe, oracularly.

"And I think she observed your admiration, also, for I saw her eyes follow you about the room whenever she fancied no one was looking, and I think there is more in it than you intend us to understand, and that you are a very profound person."

"It's time I should be," said Mr. Dawe, and the gong began to sound for luncheon as he spoke.

END OF VOL. I.

LONDON:
WHITING, BEAUFORT HOUSE, DUKE STREET, LINCOLN'S-INN-FIELDS.

www.ingramcontent.com/pod-product-compliance
Lightning Source LLC
Chambersburg PA
CBHW021038030726
47496CB00006B/1586